Claire cannot believ[...]o war.

Daniel's lips were so tightly pursed, they were white. "You're entitled to your opinion, Claire, and I am entitled to mine."

Was it possible that just a half hour ago, she'd felt protected in this man's arms, soothed by his kisses? That this was the man whose thoughts she anticipated, whose sentences she completed? The man she cared for so dearly, so deeply that she'd promised to love and cherish him for the rest of her life?

Oh, dear God, help me. Let this be a dream. Let me wake up.

But it wasn't a dream. She looked at Daniel and saw a man lacking in courage and honor.

She saw a stranger.

It hadn't taken long. Just minutes to destroy all that she had cherished and held dear.

A terrible calm came over her.

"Good-bye, Daniel. I never want to see you again."

RACHEL DRUTEN is a native Californian. She is an artist as well as an author, wife, mother, and grandmother. Much of her time is devoted to overseeing a nonprofit, on-site, after-school program in the arts for disadvantaged children, K through 5.

Books by Rachel Druten

HEARTSONG PRESENTS
HP312—Out of the Darkness (with Dianna Crawford)
HP363—Rebellious Heart
HP508—The Dark Side of the Sun
HP627—He Loves Me, He Loves Me Not

Against the Tide

Rachel Druten

Heartsong Presents

This book is dedicated to the loyal Japanese Americans who sacrificed their lives, and those who endured and transcended their circumstances; and to the conscientious objectors who served their country bravely as medics and fire-fighters, worked in hospitals and as teachers, planted twenty million trees in the forest service, and built the Transcontinental Highway.

Acknowledgments
To my still loyal and always loving "critiquers," mentor Diana Crawford, Sheila Herron, and Barbara Wilder, and my husband, Charles; to my children and grandchildren, who didn't get to see Gramma Ditti during the writing of this book; to Oma, my ninety-four-year-old mother; Noel Bryant, who likewise understood my absence; to my friends and coworkers in Tools for Tomorrow, Adelle Tavill and Judy Ware, whose help allows me to produce with less pressure; and finally to all those at Barbour Publishing, whose support and encouragement make it all worth the effort, my thanks.

A note from the Author:
I love to hear from my readers! You may correspond with me by writing:

Rachel Druten
Author Relations
PO Box 719
Uhrichsville, OH 44683

ISBN 1-59310-547-9

AGAINST THE TIDE

Our mission is to publish and distribute inspirational products offering exceptional value and biblical encouragement to the masses.

All scripture quotations are taken from the King James Version of the Bible.

All of the characters and events in this book are fictitious. Any resemblance to actual persons, living or dead, or to actual events is purely coincidental.

PRINTED IN THE U.S.A.

preface

In order to understand the passionate responses of the characters in this story, it is necessary to understand the climate of those years just preceding the bombing of Pearl Harbor. Many believed, and believe to this day, that the United States should have been prepared for the attack.

In December 1937, the Japanese army marched into the city of Nanking, China, and in seven weeks slaughtered more than 300,000 Chinese men, women, and children. One of the most horrendous acts against humanity of the twentieth century, it came to be called "the Rape of Nanking."

There was no place for the citizens to hide. The soldiers ferreted them out from alleys, buildings, streets, and ditches. The Yangtze River ran red with their blood. Babies were impaled on bayonets and tossed alive into pots of boiling water; tens of thousands of women and girls were raped and killed or forced into prostitution for the pleasure of the Japanese soldiers. Many of those who lived committed suicide. The bored troops engaged in killing contests, torture-deaths where people were buried alive, burned, frozen, buried to their waists, and set upon by German shepherds.

Detailed accounts of these atrocities were drawn from unimpeachable and eloquently chronicled accounts from the Nanking International Safety Zone Committee, whose missionaries risked their lives to let the world know what atrocities were being committed. Dispatches were printed in the *Reader's Digest* and other mainstream periodicals.

That same year, President Roosevelt signed the U.S. Neutrality Act.

In 1940, when Japan resumed its "holy war" against China, concerned Americans wondered about the scrap metal, oil, and other materials American businessmen were selling to the warmongering Japanese.

In September 1940, Japan signed a treaty with Germany and Italy, promising to join either of the other two in going to war against any country not presently engaged, a clear pact against the United States.

December 7, 1941

Plumeria-scented breezes tickled the glossy fronds of palm trees silhouetted against a clear cerulean sky. It was a bright Sunday morning on the island of Oahu.

At 7:55 a.m. the first wave of Japanese planes arrived at their targets. At approximately 8:10 a.m. the battleship USS *Arizona* exploded. In less than nine minutes, she sank, carrying with her a crew of 1,177.

The second wave of planes flew over an hour later. Within two hours and twenty minutes, Pearl Harbor was in shambles, with 2,403 American boys dead and 1,178 wounded. In addition to the seventy-seven destroyed aircraft, fourteen ships, including eight battleships, floated mangled and useless on the bay.

one

December 4, 1941

Claire Middlebrook's cheeks flushed pink, not just from the brisk November air, but from the prospect of seeing Daniel Essex III. Even the thought of him made her breathless. It had taken awhile for her brother's best friend to notice her, but once he had, she could not have asked for a more ardent and devoted suitor.

Today he was taking her out to lunch.

In anticipation, she had worn her dove gray suit—the color of her eyes—with the peplum that emphasized her slender waist and the knee-length flared skirt that showed the neat curve of her calf. She tilted the matching felt beret just so over her brow.

Of course the outfit had been way too classy for the newsroom of the *Evening Star,* where she worked as a photojournalist, and she'd had to suffer the whistling, catcalls, and teasing of her coworkers.

But Daniel was worth it.

Her dark, wavy hair swung around her shoulders as she ran up the steps of the Harper Building, into the columned lobby, and rushed to squeeze between the closing elevator doors.

"Fourth floor, please," she said breathlessly to the uniformed operator.

Across the wide, carpeted floor leading from the elevator,

tall, double oak doors, discreetly etched in gold script, read: ESSEX, ESSEX, AND MIDDLEBROOK, ATTORNEYS AT LAW.

Adjusting the shoulder strap of her gray suede purse, she pushed open the doors and strode across the plush, maroon carpet of the elegantly appointed, wood-paneled waiting room to the reception desk.

The middle-aged receptionist's thin, attractive face broke into a smile. "Good morning, Miss Middlebrook."

"Good morning, Miss Simpson. I'm meeting the Third for lunch."

"Mr. Essex is just finishing up with a client. He said he wouldn't be long."

"Is my brother available?"

"I believe so. I'll let him know you're here."

Claire shook her head. "I'll surprise him."

Down the hall, she paused by the second office on the right, knocked softly, and pushed open the door.

"Don't get up," she sang as she entered.

A broad smile wreathed Bill Middlebrook's boyish face as he shut off the Dictaphone. "Since when did I have to get up for my little sister? She's supposed to get up for me."

As he started to rise, Claire was already behind him, her arms around his shoulders, planting a wet kiss on his cheek as she shook a folded newspaper under his nose. "Wait'll you see this: front page, my photos, my byline."

Fending her off, he pulled a handkerchief from his pocket. "Oh, yuck! Sister kisses." He wiped his cheek, grabbed the newspaper, unfolded it on his desk, and scanned the headline: "PIX PROVE CORRUPTION IN CITY HALL." He glanced up at her. "So this is the piece you've been so hush-hush about."

"Not hush-hush," she said, circling his desk and dropping into one of the leather-backed chairs in front of it. "If you hadn't been so busy with your dollies and visited more often, I might have dropped a few hints."

"That's not fair. You know I've been up to my ears with the Sherman case."

"So has Daniel, but he's managed to see me."

"He loves you."

"You don't?" She arched a brow. "At least you could visit Mother."

"Come on, Sis, are you trying to slather me in guilt?"

"Of course. Isn't that my job?"

"Well, I always make it to church."

"That you do," she conceded. "It's just that I miss you since you moved into your own apartment."

"I'm flattered."

Claire crossed her legs. "Flattered enough to come back after church for dinner on Sunday? I'll make your favorite," she wheedled.

"Lemon meringue pie?"

She nodded.

He grinned. "In that case, I'll pick you and Mom up at ten thirty. How does that sound?"

"Perfect."

"Now be quiet and let me read this little gem." Bill's curly dark head bent over the newspaper. His laughing gray eyes, replicas of her own, grew solemn as he read. A slight frown creased his brow.

Claire had always adored her big brother. He was the man in the family. Their father had died when Billy was six and she only two. People said Billy looked like their father. If that were the case, he must have been one of the most charismatic, appealing men alive, for Billy certainly was. And she wasn't the only one who thought so. There was no lack of circling females who shared her opinion.

If he wasn't so genuinely sweet, he might have been spoiled by all the attention he received.

He glanced up, said, "This is great," and turned the page. When he'd finished, he neatly refolded the paper and looked at her with a serious expression. "I'm really proud of you, Sis. This took courage. Is this copy for me?"

Claire swelled with pride as she always did when she'd gained her brother's approval. "Yours will be delivered this afternoon. I want to show this one to Daniel."

"Playing favorites again?"

"Did someone mention my name?"

At the sound of Daniel's voice behind her, Claire's heart reeled into double time.

She turned.

He stood in the doorway, tall and handsome with brooding dark looks and a serious demeanor that gave clients confidence but belied his wicked sense of humor.

She thought him the best-looking, smartest man she had ever known. Vying only with her brother, Billy.

What a lucky girl, to have two such wonderful men in her life.

Daniel shut the door. "Wouldn't want to get the office all astir." His gaze locked on Claire as he strode across the carpet, drawing her up into his arms for a brief but decidedly emphatic kiss on the lips.

Catching her breath, she leaned back, laughing. "In front of my brother. Have you no shame?"

Daniel smiled, a set of perfect white teeth gleaming against his tan skin. "Why? You're afraid I'll corrupt him?"

"Too late." Billy grinned.

"You boys!" Playfully, Claire pushed Daniel away.

"Speaking of corruption. . ." Bill leaned back in his chair. "Show him your article, Claire."

Claire handed Daniel the newspaper and perched on the arm of his chair as he sat down to read it. She focused on his face for every nuanced expression as he first studied the photographs, then carefully read the text.

When he finished, he looked up.

Claire held her breath.

Relief flooded her when she saw that, as with her brother, Daniel's expression reflected his admiration.

"That was a hard-hitting, courageous piece of work, Claire." He looked over at Bill. "It appears our gal has hit the big time."

"My thoughts exactly," Bill said.

Vindicated at last.

She knew both Daniel and Billy had secretly thought her a bit of a dilettante, hired on the staff of the local evening paper more for her social connections than for her journalistic abilities. But with this breakout story, they had no choice but to recognize her as a full-fledged photojournalist.

Claire was so pleased, she was practically levitating.

"All this adulation is making me hungry," she said, turning to Bill. "Are you joining us for lunch?"

"He's not invited." Daniel's tone brooked no argument.

"He's not?" She shrugged. "Too bad about that, Billy."

"Okay, you guys." Bill thrust out his lower lip and crossed his eyes, looking really stupid. "I sure don't want to horn in where I'm not wanted." He winked at Claire.

Daniel took her arm.

In his best Humphrey Bogart imitation, he said, "It looks like it's just you and me, *schweetheart.*"

two

The air was temperate for late November, and Daniel had lowered the top on his convertible. Claire had taken off her beret, and her dark hair swirled around her head in the wind. They had driven through Pasadena and Altadena and were now up into the less populated area of the foothills of the San Gabriel Mountains.

She pushed aside a tendril that had blown across her face. "Where are we having lunch? I don't recognize any landmarks."

"It's a surprise."

"It must be a pretty remote little hideaway."

"Trust me." Daniel glanced over at her with a Cheshire cat grin. "You're going to love it." He swung left onto a narrow, winding road banked by giant oaks that formed a canopy above them. Sunlight squeezed between the branches, dappling their way with silver quarters of sunlight.

"It's secluded and lovely here, Daniel, but I'm getting seriously hungry. Okay, what's up?" she exclaimed, spotting a small sign on the right side of the road that read: YOU ARE ENTERING OAK CANYON. NO SMOKING PAST THIS POINT.

"We're going on a picnic." He grinned.

She didn't know whether to be disappointed or delighted. She'd dressed for a romantic tête-à-tête in the corner of some elegant little bistro.

"I assume, then, that our peanut butter and potato chip lunch is in the trunk."

"You assume correctly."

"Is this a test to see what a good sport I am?" He should know by now. He'd known her half her life.

He grinned again but didn't reply.

They reached a gravel turnabout at the end of the road. Daniel circled and parked, heading out.

Claire glanced down at her high-heeled suede pumps, brand-new and bought for the occasion, and noted Daniel's sharply creased, black, pinstriped trousers and polished wingtips. "You're not much better prepared than I am."

"I have to go back to work after lunch," he said cheerily.

"How did you find this place?"

"Bill and I discovered it on one of our hiking trips."

"That figures."

Daniel jumped out of the car. "You wait here, sweetheart. I don't want you to scuff those new suede shoes."

"Had I known, I could have worn my hiking boots."

"You won't need them." He grinned and opened the trunk. An instant later, he slammed it shut. Under his arm, he carried a folded blanket, and in his hand, he held an elegantly woven, rush picnic basket.

Perhaps there was more to this than peanut butter sandwiches after all.

Claire made a move to open the car door.

"Uh-uh," Daniel warned sharply. "You wait; I'll come back and get you."

She watched as he disappeared into a copse of sycamores behind a cluster of wild pyracantha dripping with red berries.

He was gone for several minutes. As she was beginning to get concerned, he reappeared.

"Just in time. I was about to go for help."

"Not without these," he said, holding up the keys.

He opened the car door and, in one swooping motion, gathered Claire up in his arms.

"Daniel!" she squealed, surprised.

"I told you that you didn't need hiking boots," he said, striding toward the woods.

She locked her arms around his neck and rested her head against his shoulder. Surrendering to the security of his strong embrace, she settled down to enjoy the experience.

After all, there weren't that many men who could carry a woman of more than five feet nine inches tall as if she were light as a feather, slender as Claire was.

The air was crisp and fresh, the earth carpeted with fallen leaves that crackled with each step. For the most part, the foliage was green, punctuated with spots of red from the swathes of fall berries and orange from the turning fall colors.

"It is lovely," she sighed.

She had to admit, despite her initial disappointment, no bistro could have been more beautiful than a setting decorated by the Almighty.

As they drew deeper into the wooded glen, Claire heard the gentle burble of a brook and looked over to see sunlight dancing on the water that bubbled over rocks and splashed against a moss-thick bank nearby. The swaying branches of a weeping willow softly brushed her cheek as Daniel knelt and, with gentle care, set her on the blanket covering a spongy mattress of fallen leaves.

An incredible sight greeted her. A square of linen on a gold lacquer tray laid with silver cutlery for two, a pair of cut-crystal goblets, and gold-rimmed china plates—even a small nosegay of white roses. There was a bowl of fruit, a thin baguette, a variety of cheeses and pâtés, mixed nuts, and a gilded box of Swiss chocolates.

Here in this sylvan setting, Daniel had created every woman's fantasy.

"Oh, Daniel. This is amazing." Her voice was filled with awe.

Looking almost smug, he dropped down beside her, his long legs stretched out in front of him.

"I'm overwhelmed," she said, clasping her hands together.

"I hoped you might be."

In the past he'd often brought her flowers and always took her hand, and he'd certainly given her plenty of kisses. He'd honed that skill to a fine art.

Then there'd been his gift of a small, leather-bound book of Shakespeare's sonnets because "Shakespeare said it so much more eloquently" than he could. (Daniel's opinion, not hers.)

That had certainly been romantic.

But this. . . This was inspired!

She took a deep breath of the fresh, scented air and let it out slowly, allowing her gaze to travel over the wooded scene and the elegant display he'd so lovingly laid out before her.

"Everything is so perfect, I can almost hear violins in the background." She laughed. "Like in a Dick Powell movie."

"Just as long as you don't expect me to break into song." Daniel plucked a grape from the bunch, peeled it, and popped it into her mouth with a grin.

"But where did all this come from?" She spread her hands.

"I called Mimi's French Chateau and said I wanted the most elegant and delicious delicacies prepared"—Daniel took her hand—"for the most elegant, delicious lady I know." His gaze was warm and compelling.

Claire could feel the blood rise in her cheeks.

"For a very special occasion."

"A special occasion?"

"Surely you've guessed."

She looked at him quizzically. "It's not my birthday. . . ."

He shook his head.

"Or yours."

Was it. . .could it possibly be. . . ?

He'd talked around marriage but not about it. He'd touched on it and then avoided it. Never quite ready to muster the courage for commitment, she suspected.

Now, gazing into his solemn face, his eyes intense, burning with love and desire, she knew that the moment had come.

Unwilling to relinquish her gaze, Daniel took both her hands in his and lifted them to his lips. His voice was husky and hesitant. Not at all the voice of a man who could sway a jury with a single sentence.

"I want us to get married, Claire. I know it seems crazy with the mess the world is in—"

"It's not crazy—"

"I've thought about it a lot—"

"Me, too, and yes, yes, I will marry you."

"Claire, will you stop interrupting? I've practiced this speech, and I want to give it. You're getting me off track."

"Oh, I'm so sorry." Claire laughed and covered her mouth.

Daniel began to laugh, also. "You're making it too easy, honey. I thought I was going to have to convince you, and I see you're already convinced. You can speak now."

"To know you love me. That's all the convincing I need."

Daniel frowned and took her hand. "We can't be foolish. We've got to go into this with our eyes open. It's just a matter of time before America is involved in a full-fledged war. We've got to be prepared. In war the worst happens, Claire."

She knew very well what he meant. Oh, she did. She did

all right, but the thought was too terrible to contemplate.

"Oh, Daniel, you frighten me." She pulled her hands away, but his piercing gaze would not release her.

"We've got to face it," he said.

"You sound so ominous."

"It's the reality."

Claire reached up and touched his cheek. "The reality is, my darling, if the worst does happen, how much more terrible it would be if we had never known each other as husband and wife."

For the first time, he looked away, his gaze following the path of the brook as it gamboled over the rocks.

In his silence, she heard the chirp of a bird in a nearby bush.

An answering trill.

She felt the thump of her heart. A heart so filled with love for him, she could hardly breathe.

He turned back to her. "I'll be a good husband, Claire. I'll take care of you, and I'll always be faithful. I'll love you until my last breath is spent."

"I'll be a good wife, Daniel," she whispered, her words almost lost in the sigh of the breeze and the sound of the splashing brook.

"I'll be a good wife, and I'll take care of you, and I'll always be faithful. And I will love you long after my last breath on earth is spent. Oh yes, my darling, I will marry you."

She leaned toward him and he toward her, until their lips touched, tentative at first, then suddenly fierce and insistent. They reached for each other and clung, desperately, until they felt as one beating heart.

three

Daniel, with Claire beside him, pulled next to her car in the parking lot of the Harper Building.

Claire touched his hand on the seat beside her. "Come to dinner after church on Sunday. We can surprise Mother and Billy with the news." She pursed her lips. "Provided I can manage to keep my mouth shut that long."

"I'll be there. What time?"

"We should be home between twelve thirty and one." She locked her hands under her chin, rocking with glee. "Mother is going to be sooo thrilled. You know how she adores you."

"And I her. Not only am I getting a wonderful wife but a great family. What a lucky guy."

Claire frowned. "I hope your folks will think so."

"Don't worry about them. They feel very positive about our relationship." He gave her a beleaguered look. "After all, you were a debutante. That makes you almost good enough for their only son."

Claire laughed. "It's just the opposite in our house. Mother and Billy think you're way too good for me."

"I doubt that." Daniel took her hand and lifted it to his lips.

❧

Claire had managed to keep their secret, but it had been a strain. At church her thoughts were so distracted in anticipation of seeing Daniel and making their big announcement that she'd gone through the rituals of the service by rote and hardly heard the sermon at all. She'd lost her place three times in the final hymn and put a five-dollar bill into the collection plate by mistake.

Oh, well, it was for a good cause.

"It's always a thrill driving with you, son." Ruth Middlebrook clutched the door handle with white-gloved hands as Billy cut a sharp corner in his spiffy red sports car.

"You girls are no fun."

Claire's knees were scrunched up under her chin in what served for a backseat. "Let's just try and make it in one piece, if you don't mind."

"Oh ye of little faith." Billy grinned but slowed to a more sedate pace.

"I have plenty of faith," his mother said. "I just don't think it's prudent to test our Maker's goodwill."

Claire glanced nervously at her watch for the nth time. "Daniel should be at the house by now."

"I'm glad you invited him, dear." Her mother adjusted her hat. "I love that boy—even if he does belong to a different church." She smiled teasingly back at Claire.

Billy swung a right onto Glenarm.

"It was a good sermon, I thought," his mother said.

"I bet you especially liked the part about honoring thy mother." Billy grinned.

"One of the commandments that you memorized as a boy."

"And forgot when you moved into an apartment on your own," Claire piped from the backseat.

Bill caught her eye in the rearview mirror and winked.

Claire stuck out her tongue.

When Bill pulled his roadster into their driveway, Daniel's convertible was already parked at the curb.

He was waiting on the front steps, broad-shouldered and slim-hipped, and so handsome that at the sight of him, Claire's heart began beating fast as a Mexican jumping bean inside her chest. If she'd been able, she'd have leaped from the moving vehicle and into his arms.

Bill pulled to a stop in front of the garage.

Claire was packed so tightly in the two-door sports coupe that she had to wait for Billy to come around and assist their mother before she could unwind from the backseat.

Daniel was already striding toward them as she clambered out.

As he drew close, the expression on his face shocked her. His eyes were dark and blazing as hot coals, his lips tight. She noticed his fists clenched at his side.

"Daniel, what is it?" she cried, running up to him.

His words came out hard and fast as bullets. "The Japanese bombed Pearl Harbor."

four

In the week following the bombing of Pearl Harbor, the newsroom of the *Evening Star* was bedlam: a cacophony of tickertapes and typewriters; reporters running through the aisles waving sheets of copy; questions and answers shouted across the room; and rumors, quotes, and deadlines. More information than they could process bombarded them.

Claire had welcomed the chaos. It meant she didn't have time to think. But now, in that brief lull between one edition being put to bed and the onslaught of activity readying for the next, weariness overwhelmed her.

Propping her elbows on her desk, she cradled her head in her hands and closed her eyes. Now the thoughts she'd pushed aside assaulted her full force.

Two days ago, Aunt Ellen had received official word that her twin sons, her only children, had gone down with the USS *Arizona*. Within hours Claire and Billy had seen their mother off from the train station in Pasadena for that sad journey to comfort her grieving sister.

In tonight's edition of the *Evening Star*, listed in small letters under "J," Brian and Wesley Jackson would be among those "confirmed dead."

Claire had caught Billy and Daniel huddled in quiet, intense discussion more than once in the past week, only to grow silent when she or her mother appeared. She knew it was not their law practice they discussed.

Both Billy and Daniel were so passionately patriotic and brave, Claire had no doubt they were deciding not whether but when they would enlist. . .and how to break the news to her and her mother without breaking their hearts.

After the family had received news of their cousins' deaths, Claire had seen a dark, determined fire in her brother's eyes, so it was no surprise when Billy enlisted in the marines. Heartsick, she knew it was only a matter of time before Daniel would follow.

Daniel, her sweetheart, her soul mate, her strength.

She rubbed her eyes. She'd never been a weeper. Never! Bite the bullet. Be stoic. That's the way she'd been raised. She remembered lines from a poem her mother had made her and Billy memorize as children: *"Laugh and the world laughs with you. Cry and you cry alone. For the sad old earth must borrow its mirth, but has troubles enough of its own."*

Those words had never been truer.

So even now, there would be no whiners in the Middlebrook family.

She felt a hand on her shoulder.

"Are you okay, Claire?" Hank, who occupied the desk next to hers, gazed down, a worried frown on his face. A seasoned reporter who'd been with the paper since the last world war, he had taken the neophyte Claire under his wing, helped her avoid pitfalls and hop over hurdles. He was rescuing her again with a paper cup of steaming coffee.

"Thanks," Claire murmured.

"Tastes like mud," he warned, "but better enjoy it while you can. It'll probably be rationed like everything else before long."

Claire took a sip and made a face. "At least it's hot."

Hank leaned back against her desk, crossing his ankles

and his arms. "Is it gettin' to you, sweetheart?"

She nodded.

"Sorry about your cousins."

"Billy enlisted, you know."

Hank shook his head. "It's a bad scene. I'm afraid it's going to get worse before it gets better."

"Why didn't they see it coming?" Claire slapped down her cup with such force that it sprayed dark drops on the copy in her typewriter. "It was so obvious."

"They see what they want to see," Hank said, echoing her ambiguous "they."

Claire clenched her fists, remembering her outrage as a college sophomore when her history professor had described in lurid detail the Japanese army's savage atrocities and slaughter of the hapless citizens of Nanking, China.

"The Rape of Nanking was no secret. It was even in the *Reader's Digest*," she said, fury fueling her energy. "What was wrong with our government? Did they think the Japanese brutality would stop with the Chinese? That kind of rampant evil is never confined."

Claire yanked the spotted sheet of paper from her typewriter and crumpled it into a ball. "With all that was going on, can you believe our president signed a neutrality act?"

Hank shrugged. He ran a hand over his balding head. "The slaughter happened a continent away. Too far away for us to be our brother's keeper."

"And we call ourselves a Christian nation," Claire muttered. "And of course the Japanese will *never* attack America," she intoned, her voice simmering with sarcasm. She tossed the ball of crumpled typing paper into the wastebasket beside her desk. "I've heard that mantra more than once."

Abruptly, she stood. "Now all that scrap metal that those

greedy American businessmen sold to the Japanese butchers will be coming back in the bellies of our boys."

Anger was easier than tears.

Standing, she was as tall as her mentor. "Oh, Hank, I can't just sit here waiting for something to happen. I've got to find a way to help. Even if it's only being a secretary for the army."

Hank's pale blue eyes studied her for a moment. He put his arm around her shoulders. "You've got a nose, girl, and talent. You proved that, if not before, certainly in your last piece on city hall. Brilliant. This old man wishes he'd written it himself." He smiled. "At your age, I had the fire in me, too. Don't squander it out of a sense of duty. Make use of it." He looked thoughtful. "I might have a resource for you."

She felt a jog of hopeful anticipation. "What do you have in mind?"

Hank had always steered her right.

"A pal of mine is an editor at *Life* magazine. I'm going to give him a call."

five

It was Saturday, five days before Christmas. Claire hadn't decorated. What was the point with both her mother and Billy gone? Besides, with eighteen-hour days at the paper, the few hours she had to spare were spent with Daniel.

This year the Christmas tree in the newsroom would have to suffice. Someone had brought in a mangy specimen and thrown tinsel on it in an effort to introduce some Christmas cheer into the chaos.

Of course there were the Salvation Army Santas on the street corners and decorations in the department store windows, which had been up since December first—before the day that would live in infamy. Christmas songs played on the radio between depressing news reports.

Everyone was tiptoeing around the season, not quite knowing how to react.

A week had passed since Hank had called his friend at *Life* magazine. Claire was sure that the man had only requested samples of her work as a favor to Hank. But she had sent her portfolio that day, airmail, special delivery. With Christmas at hand, she didn't expect to hear anything until January, if at all. The coveted jobs at *Life* were hard enough to come by for seasoned professionals, let alone newcomers like herself. For that reason, she'd not mentioned it to Daniel or the family. That way she wouldn't have to explain, and they wouldn't have to commiserate.

In the past, she might have laid the job outcome in God's hands and been patient in her waiting. Now that seemed presumptuous with all the other things He had to deal with. Besides, lately her communication with the Almighty had become somewhat volatile. She doubted He was looking on her with much favor.

One minute she would turn her anger against Him, blaming Him for the world's transgressions; the next, she'd bargain, making all kinds of promises—if He would only intervene and stop the madness. Then there were her moments of disappointment and weakness when she begged for solace in the promise of His eternal love and protection—protection she was beginning to question as the dismal casualty reports poured in.

Standing at the den window with a cup of coffee in hand, she stared out into a garden bathed in the honey haze of morning. She drew little solace from the fact that the sun continued to rise, the tides to turn, and that the sky above was as blue as a slab of unblemished turquoise.

God may be in His heaven, but all was certainly not right with His world.

She stepped out onto the covered patio, taking scant notice of the pink roses climbing up the wood columns and dripping from the guttered overhang.

She was worried about her mother and her aunt, and she missed Billy desperately, although, judging from his two letters from boot camp, his spirits seemed good.

Her own mood fluctuated. She felt as if she was just marking time.

Her one constant was Daniel.

She leaned on his strength, depended on it, clung to it. Sometimes she felt as if she was hoarding it for the day when he would not be there to support her.

That was her greatest fear.

They didn't talk about it, but she knew that the time was

growing short when he, too, would be called into service.

The thought was almost more than she could bear.

She'd managed to maintain a degree of stoicism, at least in front of others. But standing here today, alone, it was as if the rein on her control had broken. Fear, despair, and helplessness melded, heavy as a lump of lead inside her.

Drawing in a choking breath of the blossom-scented air, she buried her face in her hands, allowing herself the lonely luxury of tears. There was no one in the house to hear her or for whom she had to be brave.

With a sobbing sigh, she drew a tissue from the pocket of her sweater.

She couldn't give in to self-pity. She mustn't. She wouldn't.

Daniel would be coming soon. For his sake, she must be brave. That's how she wanted him to think of her. . .to remember her when he was gone.

Minutes later, Claire flung open the front door.

Daniel stood smiling on the porch, his hands behind his back. "Merry Christmas! I brought you something." In his right hand, he held a small Christmas tree, in his left, a brown paper bag. "I bought a few decorations from Coronet's Five and Dime. I thought we should have our own little tree-trimming party."

"What a dear thing for you to do," Claire said, fighting back fresh tears.

He gave her a teasing frown. "Why are you crying? It's not that small a tree, Claire."

"I'm sorry. It's just one of those days. The tree is absolutely perfect." She threw her arms around his neck. "And so are you. You're just the Christmas cheer I need." She gave him a warm kiss.

"I'd hug you back, honey, but my hands are full."

"Oh, Daniel, you are my hero." For a moment she

pressed her cheek against his, then suddenly pulled away. "I've gotten you all wet," she murmured, brushing her fingers over his damp cheek.

Daniel turned his head, dropping a kiss on her palm.

Claire allowed her hand to remain a moment longer, warmed by the dark gaze that read what was in her heart.

She drew him into the house and closed the door.

"Coffee's brewing," she said and led him into the den, where he deposited his gifts on the game table in the corner.

"Before that cup of coffee, I have important business to transact," he said, reaching for her.

Claire lost herself in the taste of his kiss, the feel of his arms around her. They fit so neatly, their arms, their lips. Even their hearts found a synchronizing beat.

He lifted his hand and traced her cheek with his thumb, his dark gaze holding hers in the grip of his understanding. "We're so lucky, Claire. No matter what happens, we have the blessing of each other's love and trust."

Claire nodded, catching his hand, afraid to speak, fearing those wretched tears that had been tormenting her. She swallowed and released him. "I'll get the coffee."

In the kitchen, she poured two cups, adding a teaspoon of sugar in each and a spill of cream to take off the edge. She didn't have to ask. Even in small things, her taste and Daniel's were the same.

"I got a letter from Bill," Daniel said as she entered the den. "He seems to be making the best of things."

"I know." Claire sighed, putting the tray down on the coffee table in front of the sofa. She straightened and walked over to where Daniel stood in front of the bookcase that flanked the fireplace.

He was staring at the silver-framed photograph propped between a red, leather-bound set of the works of Shakespeare and a collection of Charles Dickens. It was a picture of the twins, Brian and Wesley, looking cocky in their navy blues, Billy in the middle. Arms linked, eyes clear, triumphant smiles on their handsome faces.

"I took that picture," she murmured. "It was the twins' last leave."

Daniel pulled her close.

"They called themselves the three musketeers when they were children." She leaned back against him.

For several minutes they stood gazing at the photograph, Claire remembering that proud but poignant day.

Daniel's arm tightened around her waist.

She tilted her head against his shoulder and felt the soft, reassuring brush of his lips on her brow. She felt safe and protected. Even with the tempest and turmoil in the world around them, Daniel was her core of calm.

What would her life be like when they were separated?

The phone broke her reverie before it could turn maudlin. "I've been expecting a call from Mother," she said, hurrying to answer it.

The voice on the other end of the line was not her mother's but Hank's. "Hi, sweetheart."

Claire covered the mouthpiece. "It's a reporter from the paper," she whispered to Daniel. "Hi, Hank, what's up?"

"You can start packing your bags. You got the job."

"You're kidding."

"Would I kid about a thing like that? I just got a call from Larry. He's going out of town. He'll get in touch with you the week after Christmas to work out the details."

"Oh, Hank. Thank you, thank you."

"It's your work that sold you, not me. Gotta go. My granddaughter's here, and the family's going to pick out a Christmas tree. Life goes on. See you Monday."

The line was dead before she could say good-bye.

She dropped the phone back into its cradle and swung around.

Daniel was lounging on the couch, his coffee cup in his hand. "Sounds as if you got some good news."

"You're not going to believe it. I hardly do myself."

"Try me."

Claire dropped down beside him. "I've been hired at *Life* magazine."

Daniel put down his cup. "Darling, that's fantastic. Why didn't you tell me you were applying?"

"I didn't tell anybody. I didn't think I had a chance. Oh, Daniel, I'm so excited. It'll give me an opportunity to get into the thick of things. To really make a difference."

"That's terrific, honey. They're smart to grab you." His smile was as broad as if his own dream had been realized. "How did it happen?"

"Hank has a connection. His friend asked to see my portfolio, and voilà!"

"I'm so proud of you. When do you start?"

"I'll find out next week. All Hank said was, I'll be packing my bags."

Daniel pulled back as if he'd been punched in the stomach. "What? Don't they have an office in Southern California?"

"Oh, darling, I can't just sit here in Pasadena and twiddle my thumbs. I have to get into the fray, or I'll go crazy thinking about Billy and you in danger, putting your lives on the line for our country and me not doing my part."

Daniel rose abruptly. He walked over to the den window. Silently, he stared out into the garden, his back rigid, his hands shoved into his trouser pockets.

Suddenly he swung around; his jaw was clenched, his dark gaze unyielding. "There's something we need to talk about."

six

"I've registered as a conscientious objector," Daniel said.

"I beg your pardon?" Claire couldn't have heard him correctly.

"I've registered as a conscientious objector." He spoke with the calmness of one who had just said he was having steak for dinner.

"You mean one of those people who refuses to fight and won't carry a gun?"

He stared at her silently.

Claire looked at him, confused. He would never take such a position if there weren't something terribly wrong with him. Not her brave, patriotic hero.

Not her Daniel.

Of course! He was protecting her. He must have some physical ailment that he didn't want her to find out about.

Claire sprang up from the couch and ran over to him. She put her hand on his arm. "You must be honest with me, darling. Tell me the truth. Trust, that's what you said we have between us. If there's something wrong with you, tell me. I won't leave you. You know I won't. I'll take care of you—"

"Claire, stop!" Daniel's voice was sharp. He pulled his arm away. "There is nothing wrong with me."

"Then what is it? Why have you done this?"

"I have registered as a conscientious objector because I believe it is immoral to pick up a gun and kill another human being." His voice was low, measured, almost as if he were repeating the words by rote.

It was a voice Claire did not recognize.

A chill went through her. "I've lived night and day with the fear of your going to war. Knowing that the kind of man you are, that is what you would do. Why didn't you tell me before that this was the way you felt?"

"I didn't think I had to. I didn't come to this decision lightly, and I assumed that, since you love me, you would respect my convictions." His eyes didn't waver from her face.

She couldn't believe what she was hearing. "Let me understand. You refuse to kill, but it's all right for others to kill to protect you."

"Everyone has to follow his own conscience."

"Conscience? Or cowardice?"

" 'Thou shalt not kill' is one of the commandments, Claire. Have you forgotten?"

"I can't believe you. Using the Bible to justify this." She turned away. "Your sudden piety amazes me."

A surge of anger suffused her, and she turned back. "Who do you think you are, putting yourself up as a model of morality while our boys—my brother—are putting their lives on the line?"

At the mention of Billy, a pained expression passed across Daniel's face, but Claire was unmoved. "And while we're at it, the Bible also describes wars that are just and a God that is vengeful."

"Is that the God you believe in?" Daniel's dark eyes burned into her.

"No, I believe in a God of love. But I also believe that if we break God's laws, there is a price to pay. And I believe that we all have a right to live in peace and freedom, to fulfill our own destiny and our faith, and if these rights are taken away or abused or attacked, we *are* our brother's keepers. And when we turn a blind eye, we end up in a war like we're fighting now."

Daniel's lips were so tightly pursed, they were white. "You're entitled to your opinion, Claire, and I am entitled to mine."

Was it possible that just a half hour ago, she'd felt protected in this man's arms, soothed by his kisses? That this was the man whose thoughts she anticipated, whose sentences she completed? The man she cared for so dearly, so deeply that she'd promised to love and cherish him for the rest of her life?

Oh, dear God, help me. Let this be a dream. Let me wake up.

But it wasn't a dream. She looked at Daniel and saw a man lacking in courage and honor.

She saw a stranger.

It hadn't taken long. Just minutes to destroy all that she had cherished and held dear.

A terrible calm came over her.

"Good-bye, Daniel. I never want to see you again."

seven

Daniel Essex unbuttoned his tuxedo jacket and leaned back against the door to the solarium that overlooked the Fielding estate. His efforts at perfecting a calm facade these past few years had never served him better than today.

Absently, his gaze followed Jack and Daisy, the Reverend and Mrs. Jack McCutcheon, greeting their wedding guests as they strolled hand-in-hand among the pink-clothed tables with centerpieces of coral-pink roses and flickering votive candles.

Pink. Daniel smiled. Daisy's favorite color.

Above the lush gardens, the setting sun festooned the twilight sky with red and gold ribbons that draped over the purple-shadowed San Gabriel Mountains like a theatrical backdrop.

The music from a string quartet floated on the scented breeze, muted only by the murmur of happy voices and bursts of laughter.

Certainly, a melding of spirit and setting made this most holy and blessed celebration perfect. Almost.

As he had so often these past three days, he reflected on his own dashed dreams while his searching gaze scanned the assembled crowd for the one woman he had most wanted. . .and knew he could never have.

The thought tugged poignantly at Daniel's heart.

He found her. Alone. A slender silhouette at the edge of the crowd. He wondered if she felt as torn as he.

He studied her profile as she looked out past the rose garden to the *arroyo* beyond: her patrician nose, her full, generous mouth, her trim chin, the gentle curve of her long, swanlike neck.

He grimaced. *Swanlike neck.* That was a cliché if he'd ever heard one. But how else could he describe it?

Her dark hair was pulled straight back from her brow and caught in a thick bun at her nape. On anyone else, the style might seem severe; on Claire it served to emphasize the elegance and delicacy of her features, her wide-set gray eyes, her well-shaped ears.

She was tall. Taller than any of the other women and many of the men. And thin as a reed, but with the soft, graceful curves of a woman beneath the gently clinging fabric of the pink bridesmaid's dress falling in sweeping folds that brushed the grass.

Daniel drank her in, inhaled her essence with each breath, her elegance, her languid grace.

The past years had diminished none of it. If anything, time had only enhanced her beauty and added to her aura, character, and poise.

He wondered, would she forgive him if she knew the truth?

Would knowing matter?

The damage had been done.

She lifted a slender hand to her throat and turned as if she had felt his probing gaze. Their eyes met. Quickly, she turned away as she had for the past three days.

This was getting ridiculous.

Their paths were bound to cross whether she liked it or not.

Leaving the solarium, Daniel strode across the patio and down the steps.

❧

Claire Middlebrook had felt that telltale tickle on the back of her neck that told her she was being watched.

It did not particularly surprise her to find it was Daniel.

What surprised her was the tightness that clutched her heart. Like the spontaneous reflex from an unpleasant habit that you thought you'd broken or the twitch of a phantom limb.

She knew it had less to do with Daniel than the mood of the moment. Certainly, no regrets remained. She would always be grateful she'd found out about him in time, saving her from taking those ultimate vows that now bound Daisy and Jack.

The festivities leading up to the wedding had been so hectic that she had managed to stay out of Daniel's way, to position herself at the other side of the room, the opposite end of the table, acknowledging him with little more than a passing nod. But she knew that luxury could not last forever. They traveled in the same circles. They belonged to the same country club, and astonishingly, her mother still had affection for him.

Despite everything.

Oh no. He was coming straight for her.

Tall, handsome, and brooding as he'd ever been. Everything about him was dark: his hair, his brows, his eyes. . .his disposition. Pride carved into his square jaw and resolute mouth.

Her own pride supplanted her desire to flee.

He stood before her. "You can't avoid me forever, Claire," he said quietly.

She kept her tone equally calm. "I suppose not."

"Although, I must say, you've managed to do a pretty good job so far," he said.

She shrugged.

"How's Ruth?"

"Mother has her good days and bad. You know how it is with. . ." Claire looked away.

Cancer, the unspoken curse.

"I know," he said quietly.

"It was nice of you to visit her. Of course, now that I've come back, you won't have to bother."

"It's no bother. She's good company. I'm fond of her."

"And she of you. Although, under the circumstances, I can't imagine. . ." Claire let her voice drift.

She could see the muscle in his jaw bunch, but other than that, he didn't react.

"I'm sorry it had to be her illness that brought you home," he said.

"I haven't thought of this as my home for some years."

Silence.

"Where is home?" he finally asked.

"Wherever my next assignment takes me."

"Your magazine spread on the returning veterans was remarkable."

"Thank you."

"Who would have thought the girl with the Brownie camera at church picnics would turn into a photojournalist for *Life* magazine?"

"Amazing what war brings out in people."

That time he didn't even flinch. "Isn't it?"

Again silence. Awkward and unyielding on both their parts.

Claire gave in first. "Are you still practicing law with your father?"

Daniel looked surprised that she had to ask.

Since she'd left, she'd made it a point to know nothing about him, discouraging anyone who suggested otherwise.

"I'm a one-man firm now," he said.

"Your dad didn't—"

"No. He's still living. Retired. He and Mother moved to the desert."

She wasn't surprised. No doubt the shame had been his father's impetus. It was no secret that Robert Essex had shared the prevailing view that his son was a coward.

"Other than Dad, there's only one other partner I would have wanted." Daniel looked directly into her eyes, allowing for a moment the depth of his feelings to show.

Bill's name hung between them like an electric force.

How dare he bring her precious brother into this? A man who had epitomized all the fine and noble qualities that Daniel Essex lacked. A man who had sacrificed his life bravely on the battlefield for his country, while Daniel languished safely at home, cloaked in the cowardly excuse of conscientious objection.

At one time, the anger that simmered within her would have boiled over. She would have railed at him. Made an issue. . .probably a scene. He was one of the reasons she'd been so anxious to leave. Not to eliminate her righteous indignation, but to control it, direct it productively.

She took a deep, calming breath and averted her gaze toward the mountains.

Surely he could tell this conversation was over.

Daniel thrust his hands into the pockets of his trousers. "How long do you think you'll be staying?"

"As long as it takes."

"Don't say that, Claire. Only God knows Ruth's time—"

His words hit her like a blowtorch. Her eyes burned, her fists clenched, her self-control incinerated. "Don't you dare talk to me about God or death. What do you know? You, who didn't even bother to come home for your best friend's funeral."

Her heart was pumping furiously, her breathing shallow and fast. "What was it that kept you away, Daniel, indifference or shame?"

eight

Daniel felt the muscles in his jaw tighten. The war might be over for the rest of the world, but not for Claire. "You know that if there'd been any possible way, I would have been at Bill's funeral."

She glared at him. "Oh, yes. I'm sorry. I forgot how you pride yourself on being so *conscientious*."

Daniel looked into the face that he had once loved so dearly. A face that had reflected compassion, joy, strength, and faith now seethed with only bitterness and hate.

This was not the woman he had yearned for, held in his heart for these past years. Not the same woman at all. And looking at her now, he doubted she ever would be so again.

He felt empty and sad as much for Claire as for himself.

"Claire. Daniel. Stay right there." Daisy's voice floated over the crowd. "I'm bringing the photographer."

The eyes of the assembled guests turned as one toward them.

Or so it seemed to Daniel.

He would have gladly disappeared and could feel Claire trying to conceal herself behind him. Difficult, given that, in her high heels, she was not that much shorter than he.

"I want a picture of the four of us," Daisy called, clutching Jack's hand as she ran toward them, her wedding veil billowing like wings behind her, the photographer in tow.

She arrived breathless and smiling. "Just like old times." She beamed, and a soft look of joy wreathed her face as she embraced them both. "Just like old times," she whispered with the certainty that everything was going to be all right. No one Daisy loved could possibly be unhappy on her special day.

Neither Daniel nor Claire had the heart to set her straight.

"Claire, you stand in front of Daniel. Jack, you get behind me," Daisy directed. "Could you get a close-up, please?" she asked the photographer.

They all moved obediently into place.

The photographer motioned with his free hand at Daniel. "Put your arm around the lady."

Daniel felt Claire's shoulders tense, but to do otherwise would cause unwanted attention.

"That's right." The photographer adjusted his lens. "Hold it. Everybody say cheese."

≈

It was near ten o'clock when Claire unlocked the door and tiptoed across the hardwood floor of the entry hall.

All the way home from the wedding, she had chastised herself for losing her cool with Daniel. One would think after all this time she'd have her emotions under better control.

She was even more furious at her involuntary response when he'd put his arm around her. The warm, tingling heat that had suffused her whole being when he'd laid his hand on her shoulder and pulled her close.

More upsetting, still, was her disappointment when he withdrew the minute the picture was snapped, as if he couldn't remove himself fast enough.

Of course, that was how she felt, too. She sighed. But it wasn't very flattering, just the same.

She kicked off her high heels and padded down the hall to check on her mother as she had for the last three nights since she'd returned to Pasadena.

The bedroom door squeaked softly as she pushed it open.

"I'm awake, dear." Her mother's voice was thin and weary. Shocking from a woman who until recently had had such vitality and strength.

Claire's heart ached with the inevitability of her mother's death. Too soon. She was only fifty-five, her hair still dark. Only the deeper smile wrinkles around her eyes betrayed her age.

What had Daniel said? "God knows Ruth's time."

Had God known her brother Bill's time? Her father's, when he'd died of a heart attack before she was old enough to remember him?

"What a friend we have in Jesus. . ." What a joke.

"Come and sit down, dear. I want to hear all about the wedding." Her mother patted a place beside her on the bed.

Ever since Claire could remember, this had been their nightly ritual. No matter how late she came in, her mother would be waiting. She'd smooth the cover next to her as she was doing now, and Claire would sit down and tell her about the football game or the movie. . .or even whether her date had kissed her good night. They were that close.

Across from the bed, the window was open and the drapes pulled back so her mother could "smell the jasmine and see the stars." A gibbous moon cast the elegantly appointed room in a silver glow.

Claire crossed the room and lowered herself onto the bed. She leaned over and kissed her mother's cheek, hot and dry as parchment.

Claire's throat tightened.

"I love you, darling." Her mother patted her hand. "You never caused me a moment's worry." She lay back against the pillow and chuckled. "I can't say as much for your brother. He and that Daniel were full of the dickens when they were young. Remember the time they brought Mrs. Clark flowers?" Her mother took a shallow, faltering breath. "She was so touched, she gave them each a quarter."

"And of course they took it." Claire had heard this story before. But it seemed to tickle her mother to tell it.

"Indeed they did and hightailed it out of there before the lady discovered the flowers were from her own garden." Her mother turned and smiled at Claire. "Remember what a good sport she was? Laughed about it. She said. . ." Her mother paused, drawing another shallow breath.

"They'd either end up president of the United States or in the penitentiary."

Since Claire had come home, much of their time together had been spent in reminiscing, as if her mother needed to take inventory of a life that was coming to a close.

"I remember when the boys were in sixth grade and stole Mr. Greib's outdoor Christmas lights."

"And he called the police," Claire said.

Her mother smiled. "They were both so scared, I think that's what ended their life of crime."

"Bill's anyway," Claire amended tersely.

"That's not fair, dear. Being a conscientious objector is not the same as being a criminal."

"Under the law it is."

Claire could have kicked herself. Why hadn't she just let it drop? It only gave her mother a chance to defend Daniel.

"Don't be so harsh to judge him, dear. We don't know the whole story. Besides, he was only in jail a short time."

"He wasn't there for the duration of the war? You didn't tell me that."

"You never let me."

"Well, I am now. Why did they let him out?"

Her mother sighed. "Nobody knows. He won't discuss it."

"That doesn't surprise me. I'd hardly call him a great communicator."

Her mother sank back against the pillow. For a moment, she was silent in her own thoughts. Finally she turned her head again toward Claire. "So tell me about the wedding. I wish I could have been there. I love weddings."

Claire lay down beside her mother and snuggled close, her arm across her mother's waist. She described in detail the ceremony in Jack's church: the flower-laden sanctuary, the dozen groomsmen and pink-clad bridesmaids, the final triumphant ending when they all marched out to the ringing voices of a teenage choir singing Handel's "Hallelujah Chorus." She described the reception in the Fielding gardens, the food, the pink tablecloths, the flowers, and the music.

Not once did she mention Daniel Essex, nor did her mother ask.

nine

Claire slept in Sunday morning and did not go to church. The wedding the day before. . .seeing old friends. . . Daniel. . .had taken an emotional toll. She needed time to sort things out.

Besides, she had her issues with God—not the least of them her mother's illness.

Sleep had not come easily the night of the wedding nor Sunday. Sad thoughts always rose with the dark. Everything seemed bleaker. So Monday morning when she was awakened by the sound of a vacuum, it seemed inordinately early.

Vaguely, she remembered her mother mentioning a new housekeeper.

She rolled onto her stomach and covered her head with the pillow.

It didn't help.

She focused one bleary eye on the electric clock on the bedside table.

Nine thirty?

Her poor mother would be starving.

She threw aside the covers and slipped her feet into her slippers as she grabbed her robe from the edge of the bed.

Thrusting open the bedroom door, she was confronted by a petite Asian woman about her age. The woman, pushing a vacuum, turned it off at the sight of Claire.

"I am sorry. I didn't realize you were asleep." She spoke English without an accent. "I'll finish later."

45

This was her mother's housekeeper?

"No. Go on with your work," Claire said. "I have to fix Mother's breakfast anyway."

"Oh, I've already taken care of it."

Claire's annoyance was immediate and irrational. The servant's poise and familiarity seemed to verge on arrogance.

"I'm Mrs. Middlebrook's daughter," Claire said abruptly.

"How do you do?" The woman's dark, almond eyes gazed benignly back at Claire as she tucked a loose strand of straight black hair behind her ear. "I'm Helen Yamashida, Mrs. Middlebrook's housekeeper."

Yamashida. That was Japanese. "Mother mentioned you."

The woman smiled.

"Yes. . .well. . .since you've already taken in her breakfast, I assume my mother is awake." Claire gave a cursory nod and hurried down the hall to her mother's bedroom.

She knocked brusquely and opened the door without waiting for a response.

Her mother was sitting up in bed, supported by an abundance of soft pillows. She wore a pale blue satin bed jacket and a chipper expression. "Good morning, sleepyhead."

Claire shut the door just short of a bang. "Mother, that woman—"

"Helen." Her mother smiled.

"She introduced herself."

"Isn't she adorable? She takes such good care of me. Just look at this lovely breakfast. She arranges everything so artfully; it really stimulates my flagging appetite."

"Mother, she's *Japanese*."

Her mother gave her a quizzical frown, stopping the forkful of scrambled eggs midway to her mouth.

"Why would you hire a Japanese?"

"Keep your voice down. She'll hear you," her mother said sharply, dropping the fork onto her plate with a clatter.

Claire crossed her arms and looked down at her mother. "All right. Who set you up?"

"What do you mean, set me up?"

"The woman didn't just plop out of the sky into your lap. Who referred her to you?"

"Oh that? It was just. . ."

"Yes, Mother?"

"Very well." Her mother glared up at her. "Daniel."

"Daniel Essex?" Fury flashed through Claire. What right had he?

Her breathing accelerated; her fingernails clawed into her forearms. Turning away, she struggled for control. She didn't want her mother to see the extent of her anger.

"I knew you'd be upset," her mother said. "That's why I didn't want to tell you."

"I'm not upset," Claire said, gritting her teeth.

"You are."

"No, really." Claire unclenched her hands and faced her mother again. "I'm just surprised, that's all. I mean, under the circumstances I would have thought—"

"What circumstances?" Her mother frowned.

Claire felt the heat of bitterness flame again.

"I hope I'm not about to hear what I think I am."

"Oh, Mother, I wish I could be the Christian you are, but the Japanese killed my brother."

Anger and disappointment fused in her mother's eyes. "Helen is as American as you are. Her brother fought in the war, too. On our side. In Italy. He survived, thank God, but he left a leg in the Arno River." She pushed away her tray. "And while he fought for his country, his family was incarcerated in Manzanar Internment Camp. More's the shame. And there's enough of *that* to go around."

Her mother had always championed unpopular causes. She'd picketed against the repeal of prohibition; during the war, she had actively supported the cause of the conscientious objectors. Her devotion to Daniel had triggered that. And now, thanks to Daniel, she was embracing the local Japanese, her son's killers.

It was almost more than Claire could stomach.

But she must. Though, sadly, not for much longer.

Her heart wrenched as she watched her mother struggle for each breath.

"Take this away." Her mother fluttered a wan hand at the tray. "I've lost my appetite." She fell back into the pillows, her face drawn with an exertion she could ill afford.

In the past, Claire wouldn't have hesitated to speak her mind, but her mother's illness frightened her into silence. She hurried over to the bed. "I'm sorry, Mother," she said soothingly. "I didn't mean to upset you. But it was such a shock. You should have warned me."

"I thought I did."

"Yes, that you'd hired a housekeeper. Not that she was Japanese."

"Please, Claire. Enough."

Claire shrugged and sat down at the foot of the bed. "I just wouldn't have been as surprised, that's all. I mean, Helen is hardly an Oriental name." She stroked the mound of spread that covered her mother's feet. "Anyway, how I feel about the woman—"

"Her *name* is Helen." Her mother might be frail, but she was still feisty.

"What I feel about Helen doesn't matter anyway," Claire

said. "What matters is how you feel about her and if she takes good care of you. That's what's important."

Her mother shook her head sadly. "I tried to bring you and your brother up without prejudice, to judge people on their own merits." She took a sighing breath. "I pray I didn't fail."

"You didn't fail, Mother." Claire knelt down beside her. "It's just that. . .the war changed things."

Her mother lifted a pale hand and smoothed Claire's sleep-tousled hair. "It's easy to hold high ideals when we aren't being tested. It's when we're tested that they count. That's the measure of the man." She looked at her daughter. "And woman."

Claire averted her gaze.

"We're all victims, Claire," her mother said quietly. "Helen and her family as much as ours."

"Not quite," Claire murmured. "They're all still alive."

"Yes, but they lost everything." Her mother slid her hand down Claire's cheek and gently lifted her chin, forcing Claire to meet her gaze. "Remember that verse in Proverbs that I made you and Billy memorize when you were little?"

Claire smiled. "Which one, Mother?"

" 'Let not mercy and truth forsake thee: bind them about thy neck; write them upon the table of thine heart.' "

Claire squeezed back tears.

It was too late.

From the time she'd learned her brother Bill was slaughtered in the Philippines, she had seen truth in a different way. And mercy was erased from the table of her heart.

ten

Claire felt suspended, locked in time. Living with death was like treading water. You had to concentrate on the moment to stay afloat.

Every day for the two weeks she had been there, her mother's routine was the same. Breakfast in bed, a morning nap. If she was able, lunch at the corner table in the den overlooking the garden, then a slow promenade around the patio, clinging to Claire's arm. A brief rest and they would spend the afternoon reading or reminiscing, her mother curled under a blanket on a lounge chair outside, the weather willing, or in the den in front of the fire.

Then dinner and bed.

The next day, the cycle would begin again.

When they talked, it was mostly about the past.

"Remember when you and Billy. . .Your father and I. . . As a child, I can recall. . ."

Her mother was serene, confident that soon she would be in God's company and the company of Billy and her husband and the generations of those she loved who had preceded her to that "shining city on the hill," where they were all at peace and whole again.

Her mother's one concern, her only unfinished business, was Claire.

Claire understood that. In a way, she considered herself unfinished business.

Coming back home, participating in Daisy and Jack's

wedding. . .seeing Daniel again. . .reminded her of the dreams and joys that would never be and of how alone she was soon to become. At least she had her career. It had given her purpose. It still did.

But it had also shaken her faith.

At the beginning of the war when Claire left for Washington, D.C., it turned out to be as much to get away from Daniel as to serve the war effort. She condemned his cowardice, embarrassed by his stand as a conscientious objector.

She had thrown herself into her photography assignments, volunteered compulsively at the Red Cross and the USO. It was almost as if she were trying to make up for Daniel's lack with her own efforts.

But it wasn't until *Life* assigned her to do a piece on the VA hospital that her heart made a dramatic and irrevocable change.

There she saw "the halt and lame" in all their agony; she saw the maimed and the blind; in the mental wards she saw men, perfect in body, whose tortured minds and ravaged souls would never be redeemed.

What started as dismay turned to revulsion and hatred against the beasts who'd caused this misery. The change came when it was confirmed that her precious brother had been captured, starved and tortured, and then brutally murdered by the Japanese.

If death could be a gift, it had been for him.

How could she forget that? How could she forgive his killers?

These were the memories that haunted her dreams and shadowed her days.

These were the thoughts she could never share with her dying mother.

So for the short time her mother had left, Claire would lie. She would pretend to forgive and tolerate. She would pretend to believe that God was love and was our protector, and. . .whatever. Whatever her mother wanted, she would pretend to believe.

ॐ

It was Thursday night. Helen's night out. Over dinner, Claire's mother said nonchalantly, "Daniel called this afternoon while you were at the market."

"That was good timing." Concentrating on her next bite of broccoli, Claire made her tone equally casual, although the mention of Daniel's name still caused a tightening in her chest and a curiosity that she refused to acknowledge—at least publicly.

Out of the corner of her eye, she saw her mother watching for a reaction. She popped the flower of broccoli into her mouth. "I thought we weren't going to talk about Daniel."

"I wouldn't have, except he's visiting tonight."

Claire's head shot up. "He's coming here?"

"In my condition, I can hardly be expected to go out," her mother said with a splash of her old spirit. She put down her fork and wiped her mouth with the corner of her napkin. "I miss him. He used to drop by quite frequently." Lifting the cut-crystal goblet to her lips, she took a sip of water. "We had a regular Scrabble game on Helen's night off. Now that you're here, I guess he feels uncomfortable in coming."

Not nearly as uncomfortable as I would feel if he did. Claire took a deep, calming breath. "Mother, it's your home. You can entertain anyone you wish. Besides, he's not coming to see me; he's coming to see you. I'll just go into my room and read my book, and you two can have your Scrabble game."

"I was rather hoping you'd join us," her mother said. "It's

really more fun with three."

Claire put down her fork and clasped her hands in her lap. Looking directly at her mother, she said, "Where is this heading?"

Her mother gave a long, labored sigh. "With Daniel as the executor of my estate, I just don't want there to be animosity between you."

"And you think a Scrabble game will fix it?"

"Of course not. But I hoped that if you got to know him again, it would help. He's not what you think."

"I'm not alone in my opinion, Mother. From what I gather, Daniel Essex doesn't have very many admirers."

"I'm well aware of that." Her mother pushed back from the table. "And all of you are wrong. Daniel knows God, and he knows himself. I consider him a very brave man. It takes great courage to follow your conscience, do what is right, knowing you'll be vilified for it." Her mother moved unsteadily to her feet. "As I recall, our Lord was not always so popular, either."

Claire rose to assist her. "You're comparing him with Jesus Christ? Please, Mother."

"Of course I'm not." Her mother shrugged away Claire's helping hand. The gaze she laid on her daughter crackled with the fire of her conviction. "But Daniel prayed to God for guidance, and then he *listened*. That in itself is unique. I admire him. Yes, I do."

Claire looked silently at her mother. There was no point in arguing. Her body might be frail, but she had a ferocious spirit when it came to matters of the Lord.

"Daniel is very lucky to have you for an advocate."

"I'm lucky to have him for a friend."

Claire didn't reply.

As she helped her mother over to the wingback chair in front of the fireplace, she thought, *Mother, you can't have forgotten that patriotism has its virtues, too. Your own son died to protect the rights of men too cowardly to fight their own battles. Men like Daniel Essex.*

She dreaded seeing him.

Yet as she cleared the dinner dishes and cleaned the kitchen, every fiber of her being was attuned, suspended, waiting for that moment when the doorbell would ring. She would have to answer it, and he would be standing there, tall and handsome as he was when they were young and innocent and all their hopes and dreams were still possible. Before the war pulled them apart.

Before Claire was set adrift in a sea of bitterness and doubt.

The doorbell did ring, finally.

For a moment she was frozen to the spot. Then, with moist palms and a beating heart, she moved to answer it.

eleven

Standing on the front porch of Ruth Middlebrook's house, Daniel shifted his briefcase into his left hand and rang the bell again.

As he waited, he was filled with a mixture of anticipation and dread. He remembered the last time he had seen Claire at the wedding, the awkwardness, the anger, the emptiness in his heart once he realized the woman she had become.

The door opened and there she was, her fine features highlighted in the muted light of the living room behind her: her soft full lips, her liquid gray eyes, the swath of dark hair swept back from her smooth, pale brow.

His breath caught.

The layers of years peeled away, and in that half light, he saw only the young girl who had captured his heart.

"Daniel."

Even her voice as she spoke his name beguiled him, soft and lilting, low for a woman.

For that instant he could almost believe. . .

"Mother's expecting you."

But only for an instant. As she moved aside to let him enter, her tone became cool and dispassionate.

No welcome there.

He stepped across the threshold. "Hello, Claire. I have some papers for your mother to sign."

"You two ought to get your stories straight. Mother said you were coming for your weekly Scrabble game."

Daniel paused to let Claire precede him. "That, too," he said, somewhat sheepishly. "But I wasn't sure you'd let me in if I didn't have business."

"Of course I'd let you in," she said, shutting the door and sailing past him. "You're Mother's guest, not mine." She paused outside the den and expelled a grudging sigh. "As a matter of fact, she said she missed you."

"I've missed her, too."

He might have added, she's like family, but he figured that wouldn't set well with Claire. He would be the last person she wanted in her family.

The truth be known, Ruth Middlebrook was better than family. At least his. She had always accepted him with an unreserved love he'd never received from either of his parents. Certainly not his dad.

Daniel had never quite fit the mold his father designed for him, and then when he chose to become a conscientious objector, well, that did it. As for his mother, she was sweet but so benign she would never have thought to challenge her husband, even if she'd had the courage.

Ruth Middlebrook had sensed the chasm in his life and bridged it.

"I'm in the den, Daniel," she called.

Claire pushed open the door, and Daniel strode across the carpet to where Ruth sat in front of the fire. He leaned down and gave her a kiss on the cheek.

"He brought some papers for you to sign, Mother," Claire said with a note of sarcasm in her voice.

Ruth's pale eyes twinkled. "I told you that you didn't need an excuse to pay me a visit, Daniel."

"Your daughter just made that clear," he said. "But I brought my briefcase anyway—just in case." He glanced briefly at Claire. "I have deeds to those two apartments for you to look over."

"Very well." Ruth glanced up at her daughter. "While I'm doing business, why don't you fix us all some hot chocolate, dear. You'll have some, won't you, Daniel?"

"When have I ever turned down your hot chocolate? It's the best in town."

"I'm afraid tonight you'll have to be satisfied with second best," Claire said dryly, moving toward the kitchen.

"Pshaw. I've taught you everything I know. Don't forget the dash of cinnamon," Ruth called after her.

"Give me the papers, Daniel." Ruth extended a pale, impatient hand. "While I'm reading them, you can set up the Scrabble. . .for three."

Daniel looked up. "Are you sure—"

"I am. And lately I've been getting my way." She smiled at him as he handed her the sheets of paper. "Long overdue, don't you think?"

By the time Claire returned with a tray bearing the pot of hot chocolate, cups, and a plate of shortbread cookies, Daniel had set up the Scrabble game on the card table in the corner of the den. When she saw it, she looked mildly annoyed.

Daniel shrugged. "It was your mother's idea, not mine."

"I warned her," Ruth said, reaching out to Daniel for help as she eased herself forward in the wingback chair. "Playing with three people gives me more time to think."

Ruth and Daniel took their places at the table as Claire poured and passed the cups of hot chocolate.

"How's Helen getting along?" Daniel asked.

"She's wonderful," Ruth said. "What a blessing she's been. I don't know what I'd have done without her."

"You always have me, Mother." Claire's tone was light

but with an edge. She put the plate of cookies in front of the empty chair and sat down.

Daniel glanced at her, but she looked down quickly and began pulling letter tiles from the pile.

She's hurt, he thought. *She feels displaced.*

"Mother tells me we have you to thank for Helen," Claire said, lining the tiles along her rack.

"With Helen here to do the cleaning and cooking, Claire and I are able to spend more time together," Ruth said, studying the board.

Ruth sees it, Daniel thought

"Which reminds me, Claire, dear." Ruth looked up. "Would you mind driving Helen to church Tuesday night? They're having a meeting for Japanese families who lost their property when they were interned during the war."

Daniel could see Claire flinch. He doubted her mother missed that, either.

Interesting. Ruth didn't mention that Daniel was conducting the meeting. For a moment, he wondered if he should, then thought better of it. Claire might not be as willing to comply with her mother's wishes if she knew he was involved.

"Of course, Mother. I'll be glad to take her." Claire glanced down at her tiles. "I guess I'm first. I drew the lowest tile."

"You keep score, Daniel," Ruth said.

"Don't I always?"

"Because you were the best at math," Claire said, laying six of the seven letters across the center pink star.

"Iguana?" Daniel laughed. "It's going to be a rough game, Ruth."

For Ruth's sake they were both making the supreme effort to be affable. And for the duration of the game, they succeeded. Before long their competitive natures came to the fore. Like old times, bantering flew back and forth, spellings were questioned, friendly insults exchanged.

Finally, the last tile was placed.

Daniel tallied the score. "It looks like—" He deliberately mumbled the end of the sentence.

Claire cocked an ear. "I'm sorry. I didn't hear that clearly."

"All right. Claire won."

Claire raised her fisted hands into the air. "Yes!"

"Are you sure, Daniel? I thought I was ahead." Ruth frowned. "I think you should check your addition."

Daniel pushed the scorecard across the table. "You check it." He grinned at Claire.

Carefully, Ruth went down the three columns, number by number. With an exaggerated sigh, she leaned back in her chair. "You're right, Daniel. My daughter won." She straightened, her expression brightening. "Oh well, there's always next time."

A tense silence suddenly fell like a pall over the table. Daniel and Claire dared not look at each other.

Ruth refused to notice and began gathering up the tiles and the racks, returning them to the box. "Maybe you could heat up the cocoa, dear. Wouldn't you like some more, Daniel?"

"I don't think so, Ruth."

"Well, have some cookies, then. Look at all that are left."

"You're always trying to fatten me up, woman. But it won't work this time," Daniel said, rising. "I can't eat another thing."

Claire jumped up. "Oh my, will you look at the time? It's almost ten o'clock. Mother, you haven't stayed up this late since I got here."

"I'm not tired at all."

"Well, I'm sure Daniel is. We mustn't keep him. After all, he's a working man, you know."

"Claire's right," Daniel said. "I have a big day in court tomorrow. Still some files to look over when I get home."

Ruth pushed herself away from the table. Her cheeks were flushed, and her eyes held a fevered glint. But she looked happy.

Daniel helped her back into the wing chair by the fire.

"Well, as long as you promise to come back soon." She looked up at him and smiled. It was a knowing, contented smile, as if at least for today, she'd accomplished what she'd set out to do.

Claire saw him to the door. He had stepped onto the walk when she said his name.

He turned.

She stood in the threshold, her arms akimbo, leaning against the jamb. "Please don't misunderstand. My feelings haven't changed. But you brought color back into my mother's cheeks. I'm grateful. I think you should come back soon."

twelve

Claire was used to the snap of East Coast autumns from the years she'd spent in Washington, D.C. What might be considered a cool October morning to Californians, she found comfortable in her beige wool slacks and light-weight turtleneck sweater.

The scent of climbing roses on the columned overhang blended with the aroma of fresh-brewed coffee. Stretched out in a lounge chair on the veranda, she sipped her second cup, absently aware of the vacuum's droning hum behind her as Helen traveled back and forth across the den carpet.

In the two weeks since Claire had arrived, she'd certainly had no reason to complain about the woman's competence. She was a meticulous housekeeper, a good cook, and took excellent care of Claire's mother.

But instead of being pleased, as she knew she should be, Claire had felt redundant and out of place. After all, she had taken a hiatus from her job to come home and nurse her mother, and instead she found herself shoved aside, having to fit into some stranger's schedule. A Japanese stranger, at that.

A fly landed on the toe of her slippered foot.

She twitched it off.

At least, thanks to Helen, she had more time with her mother than if she'd had to carry the burden alone—as her mother had pointed out to Daniel last night.

Daniel.

All morning his image kept popping into her head. Probably because last night was so reminiscent of past winter evenings the four of them had spent so happily together.

The four of them.

She sighed.

Daniel, herself, her mother, and Bill.

Her loss. . .her losses. . .made her want to cry. Blinking back tears, she lifted the china cup to her lips.

No point in reviving the past. It was hard enough to live in the present.

As for Helen, the stiff politeness between her and the housekeeper had not fooled Claire's perceptive mother. The dear soul never missed a chance to give Claire a small sermon, quoting chapter and verse from the Bible in an effort to change her daughter's heart. As if the tension were all Claire's doing and had nothing to do with Helen's remote pride.

Nor had her insistence that Claire drive Helen to the reparation meeting helped matters. It was too bad, but as far as Claire was concerned, those people's losses were a small price to pay, considering what her brother and so many other American boys had suffered at the hands of the Japanese.

Claire became vaguely aware of the phone ringing in the den behind her, then of Helen's muffled voice responding.

Through the screen door, Helen said, "You have a•long-distance call from Washington."

"Did they say who it was?" Claire slid out of the lounge chair.

"I think he said his name was Larry Hoge."

Larry, more than her editor at *Life*, her friend. With Larry, she didn't have to lie or pretend. Talking to Larry was the therapy she needed.

She went into the library and closed the door behind her. Sagging into the desk chair, she picked up the phone. "Larry?"

"Hi, babe. Just checkin' in. How's everything going?"

"It's going." It was only nine thirty in the morning, and she was already weary. "How's everything with you?"

"Fine. Yesterday my boy hit a home run in Little League."

"Which one?"

"Larry Junior."

"Congratulate him for me."

"I will. How's your mom?"

"We're taking one day at a time."

"And you? How are you doing?"

"I'm all right."

"You don't sound it."

Larry's concern unleashed a sudden rush of emotion. "It's that obvious?"

"Anything I can do?"

"I wish it were as easy as that. Mother wants me to help her housekeeper's family get their property back." Claire took a faltering breath. "I'm not heartless, Larry, but she's Japanese. I don't think I have the emotional strength to do it. I can't help it. I can hardly look at her without thinking of the monsters who tortured and killed my brother." She heard the strident tone in her voice and deliberately relaxed. Quietly, she added, "But you know Mother. . ."

"Actually, I don't."

"When she wants something, she pulls out all the stops. 'It's my Christian duty,' she says. She's even resorted to implying it could be her last wish." Claire suppressed a sob. "Which may very well be true."

She pulled a tissue from the box on the desk and wiped her nose. "Kind of like the ending to a sappy movie. Only it's real life."

Larry's voice was soothing. "I'm sorry, babe. It's tough."

"It is." She blew her nose.

"So what did you say to her?"

"What could I say? I said, 'Of course, Mother, I'd love to help Helen.' "

For a moment, Larry didn't respond.

"Are you still there?"

"I'm here. Just thinking."

"That's a stretch."

"Ha, ha."

She could hear him breathing, the raspy breath from three packs of cigarettes a day.

"I have an assignment for you," he said.

"I'm on a leave of absence, remember?"

"Not any longer. I want you to do a story on your mother's housekeeper."

"You've got to be kidding."

"Get into her background, pictures of the family, etcetera, etcetera. Follow her from beginning to end through the reparation process."

"Do you know what you're asking?" Claire's voice squeaked.

"Sure. I'm asking you to do something you're gonna do anyway, and now you'll get paid for it."

"Even if I agree, you're assuming Helen will go along with it. And that I doubt. She's a very private person."

"Tell her she'll be doing it for her people."

"Her people," Claire muttered.

"Yeah. You'd be surprised. Folks are often more willing to do things for a cause greater than themselves."

"So you always say."

"You don't have to answer now. Think about it. I'll call you in a couple of days."

He hung up before she had a chance to say no.

❧

This whole thing about the reparation meeting at the church had started the week before, when Helen had asked to get off early so she could attend. When Claire's mother found out she planned to take the bus—an hour trip with two transfers—she volunteered Claire to drive her. After all, it was only twenty minutes by car. Of course that didn't take into account the fact that Claire would have to sit through the two-hour meeting in order to take her home.

Claire pulled on her gloves. "You're sure you're all right, Mother? I hate to leave you alone. We can always send Helen to the meeting in a taxi, you know."

"Not very gracious and a silly waste of money." Her mother sat in a rocker next to her bed with an open book in her lap. "I'm perfectly able to take care of myself for two hours."

"But what if you need something. Or—"

"Claire, I'll be fine." Her mother's voice was stern. "You almost make it sound as if you hope I'll have a setback so you won't have to go."

"What a terrible thing to say. Shame on you, Mother." Claire straightened her hat. "Besides, I don't mind taking her."

"Of course." Her mother didn't look convinced. She was no dummy, and she'd had thirty-one years to figure out her daughter.

Feeling a twinge of guilt, Claire bent down to kiss her good-bye.

Her mother patted her arm. "Who knows? You and Helen might enjoy each other."

"Helen and I get along fine." Claire tucked the cashmere

throw closer around her mother's legs. "Be sure you use your cane if you have to go into the bathroom."

"Don't worry. Now scat, or you'll be late." Her mother brushed her away with a fling of her pale hand.

❧

In her mother's sedan alone with Helen, the awkward silence was as palpable as if a third person were in the seat between them.

After several long minutes, Helen spoke. "It's nice of you to drive me to the meeting."

"Mother didn't want you to have to take the bus."

"I know. She's so thoughtful." Helen smoothed the skirt of her inexpensive gray wool suit. "But I'm sorry you have to wait."

"It can't be helped," Claire said, keeping her eyes on the road.

That was the extent of their conversation for the next few miles.

Claire braked as a car squeezed in front of them.

For the last day and a half, she'd been mulling over Larry's assignment. She wasn't at all sure she wanted to take it on and was even less sure Helen would be willing. But suddenly she heard herself saying, "Remember that phone call you took from Washington, D.C.?"

"From Mr. Hodges?"

"Hoge. Larry Hoge. He's my editor at *Life*." Claire braked for a red light and turned toward Helen. "I told him about you."

"Me?" Helen frowned. "There's not much to say about me."

The light changed. Claire shifted gears and pressed on the accelerator. "On the contrary. He was especially interested in this reparation business. In fact. . ." She held out her arm, signaling a left turn. "He wants me to do a story on you and your family. Take pictures, follow you through the process—"

"Are you serious?"

"That's what I said to him." Claire sped up to make a yellow light. "I told him I was pretty sure you wouldn't want to do it."

"Really."

"I told him you'd think it was exploitive."

"Sounds as if you're a psychic as well as a photojournalist."

Claire allowed a small smile as she turned into the parking lot of the ivy-covered brick church. It was surprisingly full, and she took some minutes to find an empty slot.

As Claire pulled the key from the ignition, Helen observed, "You don't want this assignment, do you?"

"What makes you think that?"

"Well, for one thing, you don't like me very much."

Startled, Claire glanced over and was held by the woman's candid eyes. "I. . . Why would you say that? I hardly know you."

"Please, don't misunderstand. I'm not suggesting you've been rude or unkind, but—"

Claire lowered her gaze. "Look. It's not personal. My brother was—"

"I know. And I'm very, very sad for you. Especially for your mother. It's a terrible thing to lose a child. But neither I nor my family had anything to do with it." Helen put her hand on the door handle. "Feeling as you do, I doubt this would have been the right assignment for you even if I had agreed."

Claire got out of the car and followed her across the church parking lot. Before Helen reached the entrance, she called out, "Would you have said yes?"

Helen paused. "It's not something I would have welcomed. But it would have been a way to get our story told."

Claire remembered Larry's words. *Folks are often more willing to do things for a cause greater than themselves.*

Helen turned and disappeared through the doors of the fellowship hall.

For some time, Claire stood in the parking lot, staring after her. Their exchange, brief as it had been, had revealed a woman of dignity and perception. A woman who was courteous but straightforward and not afraid to speak her mind.

Qualities that Claire admired.

It suddenly occurred to her that she had just been considering Helen, not as a Japanese, but as a woman of substance and character.

thirteen

Claire paused just inside the door of the fellowship hall. There had to be at least sixty people gathered for the meeting. Some stood in small, quiet groups; others sat scattered throughout the rows of seats. She spotted Helen with those clustered around a coffee urn in back by the kitchen.

No laughter punctuated the solemn murmur of the various conversations.

All the people were neatly dressed, young to middle age, and all were Japanese—except for a couple of Caucasian ladies Claire saw sitting behind a table in front.

A young Asian man glanced in Claire's direction.

Instinctively, she moved back into the shadowed corner, an alien in a room of Orientals.

Her throat tightened as it always did when she was nervous.

Funny how war changed things.

Not funny. Tragic.

She could remember as a child being innocently outraged by the mistreatment of a Japanese girl in the private school she'd attended. An ambassador's daughter, she recalled. How staunchly she'd stood up for her. That's how they became friends.

What had happened to that girl? Had she gone back to Japan? Was she alive?

Would they still be friends?

Since the war, her reaction to the Japanese was visceral, one she could not control. Or so she thought. Certainly she would not act on her feelings. She was too civilized for that, but sadly, she seemed not Christian enough to overcome them.

People were beginning to fill the rows of seats.

As she scanned the room, she realized that the very thought of sitting among them made her claustrophobic. There was a library nearby where she would wait for the meeting to be over.

But as she moved toward the door, a familiar voice called her name.

"Claire, what are you doing here?" As always, Daisy's lilting tones grabbed attention.

Claire cringed and turned to see her friend jump up from a front-row seat and run up the aisle toward her.

Daisy gave Claire a hug. "As if I didn't know," she whispered, her manner conspiratorial. "I was just sure once you saw Daniel again, your heart would soften."

"What are you talking about?"

But Daisy's thoughts—and mouth—had moved on. "We just got back an hour ago. You were top of my list to call. How is Ruth doing?"

"Managing to hold her own."

"I'm so relieved to hear that. Jack and I have been praying for her a lot."

"We appreciate that." Claire gave Daisy's hand a squeeze. "So was the honeymoon perfect?"

"Yes. Perfect." Daisy's eyes twinkled.

"The mountains are a bit nippy this time of year, I imagine," Claire said.

"You're right. We did have to do a lot of cuddling in front of the fire," Daisy admitted, blushing. "I'd hoped we could stay a few more days, but Jack had to be back for this meeting tonight." She gave Claire another hug. "I'm so glad you're here. Isn't it wonderful what Daniel's doing?"

"What are you talking about?"

"You didn't know? Then why are you here?"

"I brought Helen, my mother's Japanese housekeeper."

Jack's voice rang from the front of the room. "May I have your attention? If you'll please all find a seat, I think we can get started."

"Oh well, you'll find out soon enough," Daisy said, pulling her down the aisle. She drew Claire into the seat next to her in the first row. "Save the one on the other side of you for Jack."

The hum of voices had quieted, replaced by the shuffle of feet and scrape of chairs as people found their places.

Daisy patted Claire's arm. "I'm so glad to see you."

"Me, too," Claire mumbled, still wondering what wonders Daniel had wrought and trying to figure out how her diminutive friend managed to manipulate her into the one place she least wanted to be.

Jack glanced back at the empty chair behind the front table. "Even though we're not all here, I think we should begin."

At over six feet four, he looked more like a linebacker than a pastor.

"Isn't he just the handsomest thing?" Daisy whispered.

"Shall we bow our heads for a moment of prayer?" Jack said. "Heavenly Father, we put ourselves in Your hands, seeking reparation rather than retribution, justice without bitterness. As we struggle for fairness, peace, and harmony, direct our minds and soothe our aching hearts with Your eternal love. Amen."

"Perfect," Daisy whispered. "Short and to the point."

Claire had to smile. Married to Daisy, there was no way Jack McCutcheon would become one of those pedantic, posturing ministers. Daisy simply wouldn't allow it.

"I'm Jack McCutcheon, pastor of Good Shepherd Community, and I welcome you all here tonight. I've been advised that our chairman had a late appointment but should be here momentarily. In the meantime, let me introduce the rest of the committee: Mrs. Beemer and Miss Parrott."

He locked his hands behind him. "Let me also add that we at Good Shepherd are privileged to have this opportunity to be of service to you, our fellow citizens. We—" He glanced toward the door. "Ah, here he is. The man in charge, Daniel Essex."

Daniel!

So this was what Daisy was talking about.

Claire's body stiffened with anger.

As Daniel strode down the aisle, Jack said, "Daniel is responsible for setting up support groups such as this throughout California."

Daisy leaned over. "Which makes sense. Most of the Japanese come from the West Coast."

Claire hardly heard her, she was so mad. All she could think about was how she'd been set up. How Daniel had sat there when her mother asked Claire to drive Helen to this meeting and hadn't said a word. He knew Claire didn't want to do it. Wouldn't have, had she known he was involved.

He could just as well have driven Helen himself.

She was upset with her mother, too. But how could she lay the blame on a dying woman? Besides, it was Daniel's fault, anyway. He'd started the whole thing when he'd had her mother hire Helen in the first place.

She felt like standing up and storming straight out of the fellowship hall.

Unfortunately, she was squeezed in between Daisy and now Jack, who had sat down after introducing his friend. To leave would be to make a scene. Not that she cared what these people thought. But she did care about Daisy and Jack, who were innocent of this whole charade. She didn't want to embarrass them.

She sat, fuming in the front row, sending mental daggers in Daniel's direction, and willing herself not to look up at him no matter how sonorous the sound of his voice or how compelling his words.

But she couldn't help herself. He was too close to ignore. Although when she did look up, he didn't acknowledge her presence in any way. The chair between Daisy and Jack might as well have been empty.

Daniel laid his briefcase on the table and turned. "No one needs to tell you that a train ticket and twenty-five dollars doesn't go very far."

"Isn't that awful," Daisy whispered. "That's all they got when they were released after four years of internment." She shook her head.

Twenty-five dollars and a train ticket? The injustice appalled even Claire.

Daniel sat on the edge of the table, one leg dangling, the other braced on the floor. He shoved his hands into his trouser pockets. "Two-thirds of the 120,000 of you are American citizens. Of the twenty-five thousand Nisei troops—your sons and brothers—there are eight hundred gold star mothers like Mrs. Beemer, here." He glanced at the gray-haired woman sitting behind him at the table. "Nine thousand of your boys earned Purple Hearts. And they weren't even allowed to visit you on furlough.

"You were forced to wear identification tags; suffered the loss of privacy, family life, and customs; and lived in substandard housing with poor sanitation and poor diet. The majority of you have returned to neither the homes, the businesses, nor the jobs you had before."

He planted both feet on the floor and leaned forward. Tension built as his gaze slowly scanned the crowd, seeming to connect with each person in the room.

Claire found herself mesmerized by the passion of his eloquence. It was as if, for that moment, she was part of one collective breath.

"It is not your shame," he said. "It is ours."

fourteen

Claire glanced at the people around her. She had lumped them all together, the Japanese.

She had not thought of them as individual citizens—American citizens—who went to their jobs every day, who raised their families, obeyed the laws, and paid their taxes.

Nor had she realized how many of them had served their country.

As her brother Bill had.

And died to keep America safe.

As Bill had died.

She saw anguish and despair etched on their faces and hopelessness in their eyes.

Daniel eased off the edge of the table. "No one can compensate you fully for what you've lost. But as Christians, we are here to help you. Jesus said, 'For whosoever shall do the will of My Father which is in heaven, the same is My brother, and sister and mother.' "

In the silent moments that followed, Daniel stared at the floor. Then with a deep breath, he raised his head. "So let's get started."

Lifting stapled pages from one of the piles of paper on the table, he held them aloft. "These are questionnaires for you to fill out. They cover your education, your job experience, and your housing needs. Pretty cut and dried. But if you have any questions, Mrs. Beemer or Miss Parrott will be able to assist you—"

As Daniel returned the form to the stack, Jack motioned

him over. He leaned down and they exchanged a few words.

Daniel straightened. "The pastor has just reminded me that Good Shepherd Church also has a food bank." He smiled at the minister. "Thanks, Jack. If the folks here don't need to make use of it, no doubt they know someone who does."

He balanced again on the edge of the table, and his expression lost all humor. "Now, while there are those of you who were fortunate enough to have good and noble people to protect you, many of you did not. The legal issues are more complicated. Some of you have spoken to me about the American-Japanese Evacuation Claims Act that Congress recently enacted. Unfortunately, I doubt it's applicable in any of your cases, primarily because most of you don't have sufficient written documentation supporting your damages. Secondly, it's difficult to prove that the evacuation was a direct cause of your loss.

"But that doesn't mean you don't have legal redress.

"If you can prove that you entrusted your property or your business to partners or friends who took your profits or illegally auctioned or sold your assets, the law provides a remedy. You may be able to recover the damages you suffered."

Daniel placed his hand on another stack of papers. "In that case, these are the forms you fill out. Once they are completed and I've had a chance to look them over, my secretary will get in touch with you for individual appointments." He stood up. "Now, are there any questions?"

Daisy leaned over and whispered, "Isn't he dynamic? And so compassionate. If I didn't have Jack"—she patted her heart—"Daniel's the next best thing. Don't you think?"

"He's dynamic, all right," Claire said dryly.

As for being the runner-up to Jack, Claire had put that kind of comparison behind her when she left for Washington.

She listened to Daniel field the questions. His patience didn't surprise her. He had always been an advocate for the underdog.

She remembered how in college he had quietly supported integration, much to his father's chagrin.

His first case out of law school had been a fair-employment suit in which he represented some immigrant who couldn't speak English.

He'd won, she recalled.

But what really angered his father was when Daniel resigned as president of one of the city's most prestigious civic organizations because they refused membership to a Jew.

That little incident made the newspapers.

How could a man who had the personal integrity and courage to stand up for what he thought was right—despite the opinions of his family and the society in which he grew up—how could he be such a coward when it came to defending his country?

For Claire, the contrast made his weakness more shocking, his betrayal even more devastating and humiliating.

By now, people were surrounding the front table, picking up the questionnaires, and returning to their seats to fill them out.

Daisy stood up. "Jack and I are going back toward the kitchen in case folks have questions about food distribution."

"Can I help?" Claire asked, also rising.

"There probably won't be much activity tonight," Daisy said. "Usually people feel more comfortable getting in touch with the church privately. They're ashamed to have their friends see them taking a handout. Although, of course, that's not the way we see it."

"Then it's better if some stranger isn't peering over their

shoulders," Claire said.

As she settled in a chair in the back of the hall to wait for Helen, it occurred to her that peering over these people's shoulders was exactly what she should have been doing.

With her camera.

Larry had dropped a powerful story in her lap. But when he'd given her the assignment, she'd had no idea the extent of the problem or its ramifications. He had offered her the opportunity to document the repercussions from a heavy-handed political decision that had resulted in human tragedy and suffering, and rather than seeing the possibilities through the eyes of a photojournalist, her view had been distorted by her own limited vision and personal prejudice.

"Well, what did you think of the meeting?"

Claire jumped at the sound of Daniel's voice. She had been so lost in her own thoughts that she had failed to notice his approach.

"Sorry if I startled you," he said.

She crossed her arms and glared up at him. "Why didn't you warn me you were in charge of this?"

"Would you have come?"

"Probably not. But that's not the point. It was inappropriate and. . .and sneaky."

He shrugged. "If you'd asked, I would have been happy to tell you."

"Very amusing."

"Your mother knew. She could have said something."

"Mother has her own agenda."

"And what would that be?" He gave her a mocking smile. Her throat tightened. "I think you know."

"Is it possible she wants us to be friends again?"

"You might say that."

"Would it be so bad?"

"Friends? Never. Get along? Maybe. As long as you realize that our relationship is a thing of the past."

"Don't worry, Claire. After I spoke to you at the wedding, I came to precisely the same conclusion."

"I'm relieved to hear it."

"But we do still have one thing in common."

"And that is?"

"We both love your mother."

"We do have that," she said softly.

"Maybe for her sake we could have a truce. At least for now." His voice was gentle, solicitous.

They both knew "for now" would not be for long. It made her want to cry. She blinked back the tears that burned her lids, defying her self-control.

Swallowing, she made her voice hard. "We already have a truce. We're speaking. We're civil."

He sighed. "That we are." There was melancholy in the slight shake of his head.

He shoved his hands in his pockets. When he spoke again, his voice was flat and unemotional. "You haven't answered my question. What did you think of the meeting?"

"You are a glutton for punishment," she said, matching his remoteness.

"You weren't impressed."

She sighed. "On the contrary. Very."

He gave her an acute look. "Are you sorry you came?"

The truth was, she had mixed feelings.

It was unsettling for preconceived attitudes to so suddenly be shattered. How much easier it had been to lay blame on a collective target.

But tonight Daniel had made it personal.

Her life would not be easier for that.

She could feel his intent gaze as he waited for her reply.

fifteen

What did Claire think of the meeting? Daniel wondered. *And why was that question so difficult for her to answer?*

It was good? It went well? Even an indifferent shrug of her shoulders would have sufficed. But no, Claire had to struggle, to ponder, to analyze.

Why did she have to make everything so hard?

"I learned a lot," she said finally, almost grudgingly, as if it were painful to squeeze out an affirmative response.

Still not a direct answer but probably as good as he was going to get.

This woman standing before him was little more than a mirage of that smart, candid girl she'd once been. Just an illusive image of what she once was.

But oh, how he missed that girl.

As he gazed into Claire's large, gray eyes, shadowed with distrust, he thought, *Ah, Claire, if you could only let the dead past bury its dead. The war is over.*

But he feared it would never be so for her.

Claire gazed back, her chin high, her expression guarded but thoughtful. "My editor called me the other morning. He wants me to do a piece on what's happened to Japanese Americans since the war."

"That's terrific, Claire."

"I told him I'd think about it." She lowered her eyes.

"So?"

Could this be a first step back?

To what?

"If I decide to do it, it occurred to me that you might be good resource."

"I'll help you any way I can."

"I'd appreciate that. . .if I decide to do it."

"You have a good story living in your own house," Daniel said.

"That's what my editor thinks."

"Helen's sole support of her family, you know."

"So Mother said."

"Did you know she's a credentialed elementary schoolteacher?"

"Really? In a way, I'm not surprised. I didn't think she seemed quite the housekeeper type. Why isn't she teaching?"

"She can't get a job."

"Because she's Japanese?"

Daniel nodded. "Another injustice. She barely makes it financially—even with two jobs."

"I didn't know she had another job," Claire said.

"She works Saturday afternoons and Sundays here at the church."

"This church?"

Daniel nodded. "She helps Mrs. Beemer in the office Saturdays, as well as overseeing the Sunday school."

Claire's face reflected surprise. "Helen's a Christian?"

"There are more than you think. It's just that most of them go to segregated churches. In the camps, the only Japanese language books they were allowed to read were the Bible and their dictionary. Ironic, isn't it?"

He shoved his hands into his trouser pockets. "Besides being a good Christian, Helen's an interesting woman and active in the Japanese community. With her contacts, she could also be of help to you."

"I doubt she'd want to get involved." Claire let out breath. "She and I talked about it briefly on our way over. Neither she nor I, for that matter, were all that eager to take on the assignment."

"But you've changed your mind."

Claire answered slowly. "Maybe."

"Then maybe she would, too."

"I'm not sure I'd want to. . .given the circumstances. He working for Mother and all."

"Here she comes," Daniel murmured.

By tacit agreement, they dropped the subject as Helen approached.

Daniel smiled at her. "Any problems with the questions?"

She shook her head. "No. As you said, pretty cut and dried."

"Then we can be on our way," Claire said.

Daniel ushered them to the door. "How are things going for you generally, Helen?"

She glanced at Claire. "My employer can probably answer that better than I."

"I'm not your employer, Helen. Mother is. I'm you chauffeur."

A bit of tension, Daniel noted, but was relieved to see smile in Claire's eyes.

She pushed open the door and leaned back against it so Helen could precede her. "She's doing a great job. Mother adores her. Thinks she's quite perfect. At times I wonder why I'm even here."

Daniel reached out and held the door open, allowing Claire to follow Helen.

"Please say good night to Jack and Daisy for me," she said. "Tell Daisy I'll give her a call tomorrow—maybe we can have lunch."

As she turned, Daniel put his foot in the door to keep it from swinging closed. "Claire."

She paused and looked back at him.

"About this story you're thinking of doing."

"Yes?"

"Maybe that's your answer."

"What do you mean?"

"Maybe that's why you're here."

Her gaze met his, and for just an instant, he felt a tenuous thread of connection before she turned and ran down the steps.

☙

Two days later Claire called.

At ten o'clock, Daniel's secretary informed him over the intercom. He picked up the phone at once.

"Claire. Nice to hear from you."

She began without preamble, as if she couldn't wait to get the conversation over with. "I've decided to do the story." Her voice was brusque, her words clipped and nervous.

"That's good."

"When can we talk?"

He glanced at his watch. "I have an appointment in fifteen minutes, but I should be free by twelve, and then I have nothing on my calendar until three thirty. How about lunch?"

"I'll meet you at the club at twelve forty-five."

"The club's fine as long as you don't care about the service."

"I can't see that as a problem. The crowd should have thinned by then."

"It has nothing to do with the crowd. I'm afraid you'll be with a persona non grata. Or didn't you know?"

"What's that supposed to mean?"

"It means you aren't the only one who disagrees with my war record. The members, the maître d'. . .the waiters."

"That's interesting. Then why do you continue to belong if you're so poorly treated?"

"Family tradition," he said.

"Stubbornness," she countered.

"That, too." He was silent for a moment, then said, "You might also consider the possibility that folks will think you've come to endorse my position if you're willing to be seen with me."

"You have a point."

"Or," he added quietly, "they might misinterpret our relationship, given our history."

"Just as long as you don't misinterpret it," Claire said coolly. "Where do you suggest we meet?"

"How about the Garden Room at the hotel? It's still good."

Their old haunt. She would rather not have, but she didn't want to seem difficult. "Twelve forty-five, then. So you'll understand this is strictly business, it's on my expense account."

"In that case, I'll order dessert."

sixteen

For a silent moment, Claire stood in the doorway of her mother's bedroom. She'd been home a month, and with each day that passed, Claire had watched her become more frail.

Her mother rarely dressed anymore, rarely moved from her room. She spent long hours as she was now, propped in her chair by the window that overlooked the garden. Dozing, reading when she had the energy, listening to classical music on the radio.

Claire often read aloud to her and had begun eating her own meals on a folding table in her mother's bedroom.

Her mother wore a flowered robe with a cashmere pink throw across her knees. Her head rested against the back of the chair, her hands clasped limply in her lap.

"Claire?" She opened her eyes and turned her head with a lethargy that made Claire want to weep.

"I'm sorry. I didn't mean to wake you." She moved across the room to plant a kiss on her mother's cheek.

She could feel the bones of her mother's jaw beneath the parchment skin.

"You didn't wake me, dear. I was just resting my eyes." Her voice was soft and tired as she lifted a frail hand and touched Claire's white-gloved fingers. "How lovely you look. You're going out to lunch. I'm glad." Pulling a wheezing breath, she coughed, a dry, weak cough. "You need to get out more. Are you meeting Daisy?"

"No. This is business."

For a moment Claire debated whether or not to tell her

mother she was meeting Daniel. Her mother would interpret it in her own way. Not the way it was, but the way she wanted it to be.

What difference, if it made her happy?

There was so little time.

"Remember, I told you about the story on the Japanese that I'm doing for my magazine?"

Her mother nodded.

"Well, Daniel has promised to help me make some contacts. We're having lunch to discuss it. The magazine is paying," she added, hoping to prove that it really was business. When her mother's smile didn't dim, Claire knew she had ignored the message.

"I think that suit is one of the most becoming outfits you own," her mother said. "Plum is one of your best colors. And that little soft-brimmed hat sets it off perfectly." With an energy born of her dreams, her mother gestured for Claire to step backward. "I want to get a good look at you, dear. . . . Now turn. Perfect. . .except the seam of your right stocking needs straightening."

As Claire bent to adjust her hose, she had the wry and fleeting thought that she should change her outfit. If she looked all that good, Daniel also might misunderstand her motives.

She straightened. "Are you all right? Do you need anything before I go?"

"I'm fine. Don't worry about me. Helen's here to take care of me."

Yes, there was always Helen.

"I'll tell her I'm leaving. I won't be gone long."

"Take all the time you need."

For what? Claire thought. *Your dreams or my business?*

On her way out of the house, she stuck her head in the kitchen, where Helen was preparing her mother's lunch.

"That smells good," she said, looking over Helen's shoulder as the housekeeper stirred chicken and vegetables with chopsticks.

"What's in there?" Claire reached for the lid of the small pot beside it.

"Don't." Helen tapped her knuckles gently with the back of the chopsticks. "The rice is steaming."

"Sorry."

"You look nice," Helen said. "Where are you having lunch?"

"The Garden Room at the hotel."

"Very elegant."

"With Daniel Essex."

Why Claire needed to add that mystified her.

Helen gave her a sidelong glance.

"It's business."

"Uh-huh."

"You don't believe me?" Claire snapped.

"Why wouldn't I?" Helen extinguished the fire and put down the chopsticks. She reached up into the cupboard and pulled down two plates. "If my tone implied otherwise, I apologize." She looked more irritated than remorseful.

Claire sighed. "I'm sorry."

I'm sorry. I'm sorry. She felt as if she was always saying she was sorry to Helen for one thing or another.

"I shouldn't have snapped at you. I guess I'm just nervous. We're meeting about that *Life* article. I've decided to do it, and Daniel agreed to give me some leads. Maybe set up some contacts. That's what the lunch is about."

Helen eyed her coolly. "Daniel Essex is a nice man. You

don't have to be nervous with him." She went on about her business, pouring hot water over the green tea in the teapot, setting up a tray.

"There's more to it than that," Claire said, feeling a compulsion to fill an awkward void of silence. "Before the war, Daniel and I were engaged. This is the first time we've spent any time alone together since." Once she'd started, to her dismay, she just kept on yammering. "It's not that I have any interest in him. Far from it. That ended when the war started. But you know"—she shrugged—"it's uncomfortable. . . . Frankly, I've been dreading it. That's why I'm so edgy."

Of course that didn't explain all the other times she'd been brusque with the woman. . .for as little reason.

Helen leaned against the drain board, assessing Claire with her steady gaze. "At the library I pulled out some past issues of *Life* and looked up your work."

"You did?"

Helen nodded and began spooning rice onto the plates. "Quite remarkable."

"Thank you." Claire felt oddly complimented.

Helen kept on spooning. "The article will be a good thing. You'll do a good job."

"I hope you're right."

Tentatively, Claire reached out and touched the woman's arm. "Thank you, Helen," she said again.

"For what?"

"For making me feel better."

Helen didn't look up as she began ladling the vegetables and chicken over the rice, but she smiled.

≈

Before starting the car, Claire sat for several minutes, looking into space and reflecting on the conversation she'd just had with Helen.

She thought back on the little frictions between them, the snapped words.

They were her doing, not Helen's.

Why had she reacted that way?

Initially because Helen was Japanese, of course. But Claire had gotten beyond that when she saw what a good job Helen was doing.

The truth was, she was almost the perfect housekeeper and companion. She was intelligent, competent, reliable, and certainly loving with Claire's mother. So much so that an obvious bond had formed between them.

Claire glanced at the dashboard clock and turned the key in the ignition. She backed out of the garage, shifted into first, and turned left toward Avenue Sixty-four.

Once Claire had overcome the race issues, she saw Helen for the jewel that she was. By all rights, Claire should have treated the woman with an open and grateful heart.

So why hadn't she?

Actually, the relationship between her mother and Helen had gone far beyond the bond of employer and devoted servant. They had become dear friends, with all the little jokes and secrets that kind of friendship implies.

Claire felt excluded.

"I'm jealous," she murmured. "I'm jealous of Helen."

As a result, she'd acted like some spoiled child who didn't want to share her mommy.

How mature was that?

Looking back, she remembered how adroitly Helen had managed to keep her distance when Claire was around; the mild hints from her mother about the tension between her and the housekeeper.

Which, of course, Claire had vehemently denied.

But her mother wasn't fooled. Claire had seen the disappointment that passed across her face but chose to ignore it or attribute it to something else.

The thought now filled her with shame.

She had fooled no one.

Except herself.

Until now.

Jealousy. An ugly word that did ugly things to the spirit.

Suddenly the twenty-second verse from the eighth chapter of Acts flashed into her head. Her mother's mantra to two naughty children as she and Billy were growing up. *"Repent therefore of this thy wickedness, and pray God, if perhaps the thought of thine heart may be forgiven thee."*

Claire didn't know whether to laugh or cry.

seventeen

The Garden Room had been a good choice for a luncheon meeting, attractive with its linen tablecloths and fresh flowers but not fussy.

Waiting for Daniel to arrive, Claire sat at a table by the window, nervously sipping a glass of ice water. She'd come early, wanting to establish that she was in charge. It would be her agenda, her parameters.

But still, she had mixed feelings. Now that she'd made up her mind to take on the assignment, she was eager to get started. On the other hand, she did not look forward to dealing with Daniel. The last time they'd been together, she'd had her mother as a buffer. This time, she was on her own.

She glanced at her watch.

Still five minutes to go.

At this hour, the crowd had largely dispersed, except for a few tables of well-dressed matrons lingering over lunch or taking their leisure between sprees of shopping.

And then she saw him standing in the entrance, scanning the room, and her heart began the familiar ruffles and flourishes of anticipation.

She shrank down into her chair, furious at herself for once again being unable to control her residual response to past memories.

Taking a deep breath, she counted to ten, willing her beating pulse to quiet.

He was standing beside her. "Hi."

"Hi."

Her heart would not still. It wouldn't have surprised her if he had heard the pounding, even as he slid into the seat across the table. *Calm. Be calm*, she told herself and felt the tension ease a little with his relaxed smile.

"Am I late?" He glanced at his watch.

"No. I was early."

That was the wrong signal. Now he'd think she was eager.

The waiter arrived with their menus. "Can I get you folks something to drink?"

"Two iced coffees with cream, please," Daniel said, opening his menu.

He'd ordered without asking, but Claire let it pass.

Suddenly, he looked up, chagrined. "I'm sorry. Is that what you still drink?"

"It's fine."

So he had some automatic reactions, too. That was comforting.

"Their Cobb salad is still good here," he offered, perusing the selections. He glanced up. "Remember how we—"

"Let's not," Claire said, afraid where memories might lead.

He held her gaze for a beat, shrugged, and returned to studying the menu. After a moment, he slapped it closed. "Well, that's what I'm having. How about you?"

"I'll have the seafood in avocado."

"I thought you didn't like avoca—"

"My tastes have changed," she said, hoping he would get the point.

He shrugged. "I just didn't want you to ask me to trade when mine looks better. Like you used to do."

"My manners have improved since I was young," she replied archly.

"Thirty-one is old? Anyway, it has nothing to do with

age. In my experience, changing one's mind is a genetic thing endemic to the female sex."

"Oh, please." She felt a twinge, considering how vast his experience probably had been these past years.

Why should she care?

She didn't!

She wouldn't. . .but she found the treacherous Claire of old, the young, passionate girl who'd loved this man to distraction, threatening to scale the walls she'd so carefully constructed to protect her heart.

She struggled to bring her thoughts back to the present.

Just in time, the waiter arrived with their iced coffees and took their order.

"Remember, this is on me," Claire said, forcing herself to be businesslike as she poured cream into her iced coffee and passed the pitcher to Daniel.

He took it and smiled. "Suits me. My ego is not such that I can't accept favors from a lovely lady."

"It's not a favor. It's business. I told you, the magazine is paying."

"Which means no reminiscing, no small talk. May I ask about Ruth?"

"Of course."

"How is she?"

Claire could feel her throat tighten. "Not so good," she murmured.

"Does she know you're having lunch with me?"

Claire nodded.

"And I'll bet you made it clear it was strictly business."

"How did you guess?" She avoided his gaze and took another sip of iced coffee.

"I'd like to visit her again," Daniel said.

"I told you, you are welcome."

He pulled his napkin into his lap. "Just so you don't get the wrong idea. I wouldn't want you to misunderstand," he added dryly.

Claire put down her glass. "That wasn't necessary."

"You're coiled tighter than a drum, Claire. Why can't you just relax?"

It was that obvious?

He met her hard gaze with an unflinching look of his own. "What if we didn't have a past? What if we'd just met for the first time, say, at your mother's the other night or at the meeting Thursday? What do you suppose we'd think of each other then?"

Claire stared back into his dark, probing eyes, glinting with intelligence, warmed with humor and charm.

She couldn't tell him that his was the face against which she compared all others; his, the wit that no other man could match. She couldn't tell him that his breadth of interests and his passion for knowledge never ceased to astound her.

She couldn't tell him any of it. None of it mattered.

Nothing could change the fact that he was still a coward. Since she'd been home, she'd gotten past hating him. But she doubted she could ever forgive him, and certainly she would never respect him.

He sat back, leaning his elbows on the arm of his chair. "You can't think of one positive thing to say about me?"

"You're attractive?"

Handsome, if the truth were told.

"That's a good start." He grinned.

"And you're smart."

"Maybe now is a good time to stop. Two out of two isn't bad. Are you interested in my first impression? I'm going to tell you anyway."

He leaned forward. "I'm struck by your beauty. . . ." His gaze scanned her face. "Your intelligence, your ambition." He paused but continued to study her. "But there's something about you that's. . .removed. . .distant. I find it compelling but a bit intimidating."

"You intimidated? That will be the day."

"You're not playing the game," he said. "Remember, we have no past."

Claire had had enough. "I don't want to play this game. We do have a past, and we can't pretend we don't."

The waiter came then and placed their salads in front of them.

"Besides, we're not here to play games. We're here to discuss the piece I'm doing on the Japanese that you kindly offered to assist me with." She picked up her fork.

He returned her rebuff with silence. Then he said, "You're right, Claire."

She saw regret in his eyes and then acquiescence, as if he was thinking, *Why bother?*

Instead of feeling relieved, as she would have expected, she felt sorry.

"No levity," he said. "This is serious business."

For several minutes, Claire picked at her salad in silence.

Finally, Daniel said, "Tell me how you see the story evolving, and then I'll know better how to help you."

"I'll need to set up interviews." She pushed her plate back and wiped the corner of her mouth with her napkin. "Of course, with accompanying photographs." She put her elbow on the arm of the chair and her chin on her fist, thinking aloud as she spoke. "Possibly incorporate old photos of homes or businesses that they've lost. . .pictures of family members, perhaps juxtaposed against shots of the camp." She looked up at him. "I'd like to visit Manzanar if I can. Take pictures of it as it is today."

"I can arrange that," Daniel said. "And of course, I shouldn't have any trouble lining up interviews for you."

"I'd be grateful."

"But I still think Helen would be your best bet—if you can convince her and her family to do it. Their experience incorporates what happened in so many Japanese American families. Paul, Helen's younger brother, served in the all–Japanese American 442nd Regimental Combat Team, you know. It was the most decorated combat unit for its size and length of service in U.S. military history."

"Really."

Daniel nodded. "The tragedy was that many of those boys weren't even allowed to visit their families when they were on leave, the government was so paranoid about Japanese spies. Interestingly, there isn't one documented case to substantiate that fear."

"I should be taking notes talking to you," Claire said.

"I've learned a lot since I started working with these people. You couldn't find better Americans." Daniel shook his head. "The prejudice they suffered before and during the war—even now—is unconscionable." He looked up at her. "That's why I'm willing to do anything I can to help them—to help you—tell their story."

"I appreciate that, Daniel. I really do." Claire dropped her hands into her lap. "I wish I could convince Helen."

"Do you think it would help if I gave it a shot?"

"Certainly wouldn't hurt."

It wouldn't hurt either that Claire was determined to turn over a new leaf when it came to their housekeeper.

And not just for a story. She hoped Helen would believe that.

When they'd finished, the waiter began clearing their plates. "More iced coffee?"

Claire shook her head. "No, thank you."

"Nor I," Daniel said.

"Dessert?"

"None for me," Daniel said.

"What's chocolate?" Claire asked, allowing a smile in his direction.

"Dare I say that sounds familiar?" he ventured.

Holding a plate in either hand, the waiter rattled off, "German chocolate cake, pot de crème, and chocolate ice cream."

"Mmm. . ."

"Hard choice, isn't it?" Daniel smiled.

In the old days, she would have chosen the pot de crème and made him order the German chocolate cake, and they would have shared.

But that was the old days.

"The pot de crème, please."

"You're such a willow," Daniel said. "It has always mystified me how you could afford these caloric indulgences and not have them show."

"You're sure you don't want the cake?"

Chocolate had always made her feel magnanimous.

"You're paying?"

"That's what I said."

"Then why not?" He turned to the waiter. "And bring two forks."

eighteen

Daniel slid the sleek blue Buick convertible, his one extravagance, along the curb in front of Claire's home and came to a stop.

Their lunch the other day had ended on a more upbeat note than he'd thought possible. Her proclivity for chocolate had done the trick. She'd even squeezed out a smile when he'd asked the waiter for two forks.

Those last few minutes had almost felt like old times.

Her bitterness was still there, just beneath the surface. But he'd also sensed a vulnerability in her and a deep sadness that broke his heart.

He didn't want to care so much, but he couldn't seem to help it. The past clung to them both like a blanket, but one that could not keep out the cold.

They'd parted with his promise to talk to Helen the next time he visited her mother. Which was what he was about to do, four days later.

As he strode up the walk, the scent of winter-blooming honeysuckle reminded him of years past when he'd trod the same path, and the tall, winsome girl that he loved so much had always greeted him with a smile and open arms.

He rang the bell.

Helen answered.

At least he got the smile.

"Come in. They're expecting you." She moved aside, closing the door behind him. "They'll be a few minutes; Claire's helping her mother get ready. You know Ruth. She's of the old school. She always tries to look her best. Even when she's so weak she can hardly lift her hand." Helen sighed. "Even for us. She says it makes her feel better." She shook her head sadly. "It's so touching."

"She's a valiant lady," Daniel said, following Helen into the family room.

"That she is." Helen led him into the kitchen. "I'm making tea."

He hitched himself onto a stool at the worktable in the center, where she had already set a tray with cups and saucers and napkins, leaving space for a teapot.

"Those look good," he said, eyeing a plate of brownies.

"Help yourself. The tea will be ready in a minute."

Breaking off a corner of a brownie, he popped it into his mouth, savoring the rich, chocolate taste. "Delicious."

"Claire made them."

He chuckled. "I might have known."

Helen brought the steeping tea from the stove and poured him a cup. "Sugar and cream?"

"No, thanks," he said with an appreciative smile. "How's Ruth doing?"

"It's heartbreaking. She's just deteriorating before our eyes. It takes both of us to give her the care she needs. Otherwise, I'm sure she'd have to be in the hospital."

"I can't believe it. I just saw her a week and a half ago. She was frail, but nothing like you describe."

"Well, be prepared." Helen came around the table and picked up the tray. She carried it into the den.

Daniel followed with his cup and the plate of brownies, setting them next to the tray on the coffee table. He sat down in the armchair flanking the fireplace. "How are you and Claire getting along?"

"Actually, very well." Helen lowered herself onto the couch and poured a cup of tea for herself. "I couldn't have said that two weeks ago. For some reason, I got the feeling she resented me."

Daniel didn't dispute her assessment.

"But in the last couple of weeks, we've become. . .I think I can honestly say we've become friends." Helen took a sip of tea. "She's a wonderful daughter, you know, loving, attentive. So patient."

"That's what she says about you."

"That's good to hear. She's certainly treating me now as if she thinks so."

Helen glanced toward the hall. "But I worry about her. There are times when she seems so distracted. As if mentally she's gone to another place. Of course, with her brother dying and now her mother, it's a lot. . . . But I get the feeling that it's something else. More. . .it's a melancholy that's deep in her bones."

Daniel's stomach tightened. He put the teacup back into its saucer on the table. He well knew the cause of her underlying sorrow. Suddenly, inexplicably, he felt a surge of anger. Anger at Claire for letting it come to this. When Bill had died, when they'd needed each other's comfort, she had already closed the door of her heart. And locked it. She'd ruined both their lives.

He put his elbow on the arm of the chair and covered his eyes with his lifted hand. He felt shame for this surge of rage that, up until now, he'd managed to suppress.

Of all times for him to allow these feelings to surface, when Claire was going through so much. Now, more than ever, she needed his compassion.

He glanced up to see Helen looking at him with a puzzled expression.

"Sorry," he mumbled. "Her brother was my best friend, and Ruth has been like a mother. It's a tough time."

"I understand."

But he knew she didn't.

Even he had trouble understanding.

For a time they sat silent in their own thoughts, staring into the fire.

Finally Daniel said, "Has Claire talked to you recently about the article she's doing?"

"The day you two had lunch."

"I suggested that she should consider using your family's story."

"She mentioned that once before. But at that time neither of us was that enthusiastic."

"How do you feel about it now?"

"I don't know."

"Your family is such a great example not only of how the Japanese suffered but, more important, of how they endured."

"There were so many like us."

"That's the point. You're a microcosm of what happened. Immigrant parents making a life in America, their daughter becoming a teacher, their son in the military." Daniel leaned forward. "Claire's committed to this story, Helen. She'll do a good job."

"I have no doubt about that." Helen put down her cup. "It's just that my parents and Paul have already suffered so much. Reliving it would be like opening a wound and twisting a knife in it. I can't see my brother as the paraplegic poster boy."

Helen's normally tranquil expression hardened. "Do you know that in some divisions those brave young soldiers were never promoted? They went into the army as privates, and they came out as privates."

Behind her, Claire said, "That's why the story has to be told." Entering the room, she walked over to the couch and rested her hand on Helen's shoulder. "I want to do it with you, Helen. We'll work together."

Helen laid her hand over Claire's. After a moment, she looked up. "I can't promise that my family will agree, but I'll ask them."

Claire leaned down and pressed her cheek against Helen's.

A small sliver of hope squeezed into Daniel's heart.

nineteen

"Mother's ready to see you," Claire said.

As Daniel followed her down the hall to her mother's bedroom, he was struck by how exhausted she looked.

Usually impeccably groomed, her thick, brown hair was caught indifferently at the nape of her neck. Circles shadowed her gray eyes, red-rimmed from fatigue. Or tears. Or both. Even her lithesome body drooped from weariness.

But if he was moved by Claire's appearance, it was nothing compared to the shock of seeing Ruth.

In the dim light, she lay in the large, four-poster bed, almost lost in the soft pillows against which she was propped. Her fingers, thin as twigs, twitched nervously on the flowered quilt that covered her.

"Daniel. Dear friend, come in," she said, her voice whispery as a breeze ruffling dry leaves.

Daniel's heart pounded as he crossed to her. The room felt airless and too warm, with the cloying scent of flowers melding with the pungent smell of dying.

He sat down on the edge of the bed and lifted her hand. It was light as a dead bird, all bones and softness as he stroked it. "Oh, my dear," was all he could manage.

"Don't feel sad," Ruth said.

The lace ruffle of her bed jacket hung loose at her throat, the cords of her neck prominent beneath a translucent sheath of skin.

Her eyes were dark caverns in the gaunt shadow of her past beauty. But her hair was perfectly coiffed, and there was blush on her cheeks and color on her lips, testament to her dignity and to Claire's loving ministrations.

"Claire—"

"What is it, Mother?" Claire moved to the side of the bed.

"A cup of tea," Ruth whispered.

"It'll just take a minute."

As soon as Claire left the room, Ruth drew Daniel closer. "When I'm gone, you'll take care of her, won't you, Daniel? Promise me."

Claire, let him take care of her? That would be the day. "You don't need to worry about that daughter of yours. She's as strong and independent as her mother." He smiled.

"No, she's not." Ruth drew a shuddering breath. "Not emotionally. Not since the war. . .since Billy. . ." Her voice faded to a sigh. "She'll have no one when I'm gone."

She began a paroxysm of coughing and reached for a tissue from the bedside table. "She's so alone." Ruth's voice faltered again, and she sank back into the pillows. Her eyes closed.

Alone out of choice, Daniel knew.

For several minutes, she seemed to have drifted off. Then her lids fluttered and opened. Laboring for each breath, she struggled to speak. "You're the only one. . ."

She clutched Daniel's hand, her eyes glittering with fevered intensity. "Be patient with her. . .if you love her. . . promise me—"

"Promise you what, Mother?" Claire crossed the room, carrying a small tray with a teapot, cup, and saucer on it, which she set on the bedside table. "I've brought you your tea."

Daniel started to rise, but Ruth would not let go of his hand. He was surprised by the strength of her grasp.

Claire lifted the cup to her mother's lips. For one sip Ruth obliged, then turned her head away.

"That's all you want? You should drink it, Mother," she pleaded. "You'll get dehydrated."

Ruth shook her head.

Claire sighed and looked at Daniel. "Why did she even ask me to bring it?" she said softly.

Daniel knew why. Only with Claire out of the room had Ruth been able to tell him what was in her heart. He wondered how Claire would have reacted had she heard her mother's plea.

He could imagine.

Ruth might not think her daughter strong and independent. Daniel had no doubt Claire would say otherwise.

He sided with Ruth.

But what did it matter?

Sadly, he was the last person Claire would turn to for solace.

Would he take care of Claire?

Fortunately, she'd interrupted before he'd had to answer. Even to a dying woman, he wouldn't have been able to lie.

He would see that Claire was taken care of.

That was different.

Ruth's hand grew limp in his. He held it until he knew she was asleep, then gently he returned it to the flowered quilt.

Helen had already retired to her room when Claire walked him down the hall to the front door.

"What was it my mother made you promise?" She stood with her hand on the knob.

Daniel shrugged. "Nothing important."

"Daniel."

He smiled. "Certainly you wouldn't want me to be in violation of the attorney-client privilege?"

"Oh, please!" Claire crossed her arms. "Certainly I *would*."

For a moment he debated.

"Well?" she said.

He'd give her the half version.

"She just wanted me to watch out for you."

"That's all?"

He nodded.

"What did you say?"

"I told her you were a strong, independent woman like she is, and you'd be fine."

"Yes. Well that's true." Claire glanced away. "I'll be fine."

He watched her struggle for composure. He knew she'd been holding on for the final weeks of her mother's illness, being strong for her sake. Now that the end was near, he could see Claire beginning to crumble.

Lines of fatigue etched her face. Her lips trembled. Her eyes were haunted with sadness.

As a friend, the most natural thing would have been to reach out to her, console her.

But the way she held her back so stiff, her arms folded tightly across her breast, told him more than words that she would not welcome his comfort.

When Ruth died three days later, Daniel was taken completely by surprise.

He was the first one Claire called.

twenty

It had been automatic. So automatic that for an instant Claire had been startled to hear Daniel's voice on the other end of the line.

"Daniel Essex here."

"Mother's gone."

"Oh, Claire, I'm so sorry. When?"

"This morning. She died in her sleep."

"I'm coming over," Daniel said, then paused. "May I?"

"I was hoping you would," she admitted.

"I'll be there within a half hour."

Claire returned the phone to its cradle with a sense of relief.

As she stood in the window of the den, looking out at the rain, she thought of how much Daniel had loved her mother and she him. For her, he'd been the nearest thing to a son since Bill died.

More than anyone else, even Claire's dearest friend, Daisy, he understood the sadness in her heart.

Claire loved the rain. She always had, even as a child. She loved hearing the *plunk, plunk* of drops dripping from the eaves onto the patio and the shimmering brightness of foliage in the shrouded mist, the fresh, clean scent of wet grass.

On this, of all days, it was as if the earth were being cleansed with God's tears.

Lately, her reactions to Daniel had confused her, and she had the vague, unsettled feeling that a motive other than his devotion to her mother had caused her to dial his number.

But right now, that didn't seem to matter.

His voice had brought her comfort.

"I've made some tea," Helen said, setting a tray on the coffee table in front of the fireplace.

"You and your tea." Claire smiled, dropping onto the couch. "Join me."

Helen poured them each a cup and sat down next to her. "There's something about a cup of tea that's comforting at times like this," she said. "A cup of coffee just doesn't do it."

For several minutes they sat in silence, staring into the flames, listening to the crackle and spit of the burning logs, and thinking their own thoughts.

"I'd better call Daisy," Claire remembered. "Jack'll be doing the funeral, of course." She sighed. There weren't really any other people she cared to talk to. She realized how few friends she still had here in California.

Now that her mother was gone, after she'd completed her assignment on the Japanese, she'd probably move back to Washington. Other than Daisy and Jack and now Helen, she had little reason to stay.

She pushed Daniel from her mind.

"I'll call your mother's friends if you'll give me a list," Helen said.

Claire patted her knee. "You've been such a blessing both to Mother and to me. I don't know what we would have done without you."

Helen smiled. "The blessing goes both ways."

Claire was about to call Daisy when the doorbell rang. "I'll get it. I'm sure it's Daniel."

"I'll make another pot of tea," Helen said, disappearing into the kitchen.

Daniel stood in the doorway; his wet hair shone silver in

the muted light. Drops of water ran down his face, catching on his lashes. His belted trench coat was spotted with raindrops, the shoulders stained dark from the deluge.

Up until that moment, Claire had held her emotions in check. She had, in fact, wondered why she'd felt so calm and in control.

But the sight of Daniel, the comforting bulk of him, the sad, understanding expression in his eyes shredded her reserve, and the first tears since her mother's death streamed down her cheeks.

His arms were around her; her head pressed against the rough, damp fabric of his coat. Through her sobs, she could not understand the words of comfort that he murmured but felt the soft caress of his breath against her cheek.

All she knew was that, in the warmth of his embrace, she felt safe and protected.

Slowly, her sobs subsided. But for several minutes she remained in his arms, leaning into him, remembering his strength.

Finally, she pulled back and felt his caressing hand gently wipe the dampness from her cheeks.

"My dear Claire, I am so sorry. I don't know what to say."

"I know." She sighed, a latent sob catching in her throat as she drew him into the house and closed the door.

Taking his trench coat, she suddenly felt abashed over the familiarity she'd allowed and for an awkward moment was at a loss, unsure of what to say.

Gently, he lifted her chin, forcing her to meet his gaze. "Don't feel embarrassed. You're supposed to cry."

It wasn't her tears that embarrassed her, nor that she had allowed him to comfort her. It was her response to his comfort; it was the melting and longing that suffused her.

It was her neediness.

"Helen's making tea," she said, throwing his coat over her arm. "I'll hang this up to dry out."

He followed her as far as the den, where she continued on through the kitchen and out to the back porch.

There, she clutched the coat in her arms and leaned against the wall, tears threatening again.

She felt guilty and ashamed. Even in this moment of deepest grief, she had responded to Daniel in a way that had nothing to do with losing her beloved mother.

She had responded to him as a man.

Her body had remembered what her heart denied.

"Are you all right?"

Claire's eyes snapped open.

Daniel stood in the kitchen doorway, looking worried.

"I'm fine," she mumbled, turning away and sliding the coat onto a hanger.

"You're sure?"

She nodded and turned back.

"Before I came, I called Jack. I hope that was all right."

"That's fine." She slid past him into the kitchen. "I was about to telephone Daisy, myself."

Keeping her eyes downcast, she moved into the den. She would get past this acute awareness of him. It was because she was so worn out from holding her emotions in check for so long, not wanting to burden her mother with her own grief. She was vulnerable, that was all. Any act of kindness would have unraveled her.

Only a temporary aberration.

"They should be here soon," Daniel said quietly.

"That's good. We have to talk about the. . ." She swallowed. "We have to discuss the funeral."

From the kitchen, Helen called, "I'm making sandwiches. You'll stay for lunch, won't you, Daniel?"

Claire looked at him then. "You will stay?"

He nodded.

"Make enough for Daisy and Jack, too, please, Helen." As she spoke, the doorbell rang again.

"Let me," Daniel said, urging Claire onto the couch.

She was grateful for the respite, a moment to collect herself.

She could hear her friends' voices at the door, and then Daisy was hugging her, all bouncing blond curls and sad smile, smothering her with the love and affection that only a best friend could.

"Oh, my precious girl. My heart breaks for you." She plopped down on the couch next to Claire. "It just seems so hard to believe."

Daniel stood in front of the fireplace while Jack got down on one knee in front of Claire. Taking her hands in his, he looked directly into her eyes with an expression of compassion and strength. Who could not trust this devout man?

"I weep for you, Claire," he said, "but not for Ruth. Right this very minute, as we're talking here, she's in the midst of a joyous reunion with your brother, Bill, and your father. You do believe that, don't you?"

He spoke with the assurance that she did.

Claire nodded, not having the heart to admit her uncertainty.

Yet if the Almighty was the source of all that is good, and if, as her mother believed, the Bible was inspired by truth and these promises were written there, why couldn't she believe it, too?

"At last, she's free from pain and worry and all earthly

suffering," Jack continued. "It says in the Bible, 'For thou hast delivered my soul from death, mine eyes from tears, and my feet from falling.' "

"That's beautiful, Jack." Claire pondered his words. "Where would I find that verse?"

He gave her hands a squeeze and stood up. "It's the eighth verse of Psalm 116."

"Could we use it in her eulogy?"

"I don't see why not."

"Mother talked to me about her service before she died. Of course she wants you to do it." Claire mustered a smile. "As long as you keep it short and simple."

"My trademark." Jack returned her smile. "Daisy wouldn't have it otherwise."

Claire looked at Daisy. "And Mother wanted the teen choir that sang at your wedding. Would that be possible?"

Daisy frowned. "I know they'd want to, but they don't have a very large repertoire. Right now it's limited pretty much to the songs from our wedding. 'Oh Promise Me,' 'The Lord's Prayer,' and the 'Hallelujah Chorus.' "

"I think we can do without 'Oh Promise Me.' " Claire smiled and wiped her eyes with a tissue. " 'The Lord's Prayer' is certainly appropriate." She glanced at Jack. "And if we're to believe that Mother's in the midst of a joyous reunion, I think the 'Hallelujah Chorus' would be perfect."

Daisy tilted her head, a thoughtful frown furrowing her pretty brow. "It makes sense to me. Why not? What do you think, Daniel?"

"I'm in favor of whatever Claire wants," Daniel answered. "Ruth also loved 'Amazing Grace.' "

Daniel knew her mother so well. So many things they shared, so many memories, so many. . .

"You're right," Daisy said. "What's a funeral without 'Amazing Grace'?" She frowned again but this time with concern. "I don't know if they can sing that."

"I heard a girl in church one Sunday. Remember that, Jack?" Daniel said. "A rather plump girl with a pretty face. She sang it a cappella."

Daisy bounced back against the embroidered cushion. "I remember that Sunday. It was Betty. As a matter of fact, Ruth commented on how touched she was. She said it was so beautiful it made her cry. . . . Oh dear."

Claire patted her friend's hand and smiled, hoping to put her at ease. "Don't worry, Daisy dear. If Mother cries, we'll never know it. She wants a closed casket."

twenty-one

The drenching rain that had persisted for days stopped at three o'clock on the afternoon of the funeral as if on cue. The clouds parted, and the sun's rays bathed the spire of the Good Shepherd Church in a halo of gold.

"Will you look at that," Daniel said, helping Claire out of the limousine.

"As if God is offering His own personal blessing," she murmured.

"Doesn't He always?"

Daniel took her arm and guided her up the front steps and through the friends gathered at the entrance for her mother's funeral. They reached out as she passed, murmuring condolences or just offering a compassionate smile. They had loved her mother, and now their love spread over Claire, filling her heart with the fullness and purity of the rain-scented air.

Many of the faces she recognized; more she did not.

Had it been that many years since she was part of her mother's life?

As she and Daniel stepped into the cool, muted light of the sanctuary, a medley of her mother's favorite hymns filled the solemn quiet.

Claire saw that the pews were almost full. These were her mother's friends, people whose lives she had touched and who now mourned her passing.

Feeling the sting of tears, she clung to Daniel's arm. It was not the first time during this ordeal that she'd been grateful for his support.

As they made their way down the center aisle, he covered her trembling hand with his and leaned toward her, whispering soothing words of comfort.

She doubted, had the situation been reversed, she would have been as good a friend to him as he was to her. It was for her mother's sake, she knew, but still she was thankful.

Seated in the first pew, her aching heart filled with the poignancy and beauty of it all: the music, the flowers, the blessings of sunlight.

The chancel was a bower of blossoms picked from the Fielding estate, then arranged by Daisy and her sister-in-law, Rebecca. In front, on an easel beside the closed casket, stood a beautiful oil portrait of Claire's mother, painted in her prime by Daisy's artist brother, Court.

As promised, the funeral was short and sweet.

Jack gave a brief but eloquent eulogy that described the life and influence of a woman who had lived her faith. Daniel read the Twenty-third Psalm, "The Lord is my shepherd. . . ," reminding them of God's promise not only for her mother but for them all. Members of the teenage choir sang their hearts out, and plump Betty's beautiful and heartfelt a cappella rendition of "Amazing Grace" left not a dry eye in the church.

"Just as Ruth would have wanted," Daisy murmured, patting Claire's hand at the final amen.

The sun had disappeared, and a misty rain greeted the mourners as they left the cemetery after the burial, but the weather discouraged no one from gathering at the Middlebrook home for the reception following the service.

The day before, as Claire had arranged the etched sterling tea service and her mother's delicate Minton china and Waterford crystal goblets on the Irish linen tablecloth, she could feel her mother directing her hands and almost hear her voice from childhood. "It's just as easy to make things lovely, dear, if only for the sake of your own soul."

Claire had smiled. Those words would haunt her.

All these beautiful things were hers now.

What would she do with them?

Put them in storage, she supposed, when she sold the house. Her lifestyle hardly accommodated such elegance.

While they were at the church, Helen had arranged the buffet with platters of fresh fruit, plates of elegant hors d'oeuvres, and a variety of beautiful and delicious pastries contributed by Daisy and Rebecca, renowned among friends for their culinary skills.

The rooms of the house were soon filled with the subdued murmur of friends reminiscing and spurts of soft laughter that had been missing in this home these last days. Although they had gathered to mourn her mother's death, those who loved her had also come to celebrate her life. There were more happy memories than sad, and it seemed to Claire that, in a strange way, there was more joy than sorrow.

It was after dark by the time the guests departed. Only Jack, Daisy, Daniel, and, of course, Helen remained seated in the den in the same places they'd sat the day her mother died: Daisy, Claire, and Helen on the couch facing the fireplace, the men in the chairs that flanked it, Jack on the left with his feet on a footstool, Daniel on the right. The fire blazed and crackled between them, sending off the sweet scent of pine.

Claire slipped out of her shoes and tucked her feet under her, leaning back into the soft cushions of the couch. She was weary to the bone but strangely exhilarated. All the love swirling around her had served to buoy her spirits rather than depress her, as she'd expected.

Especially the love from those in this room.

She had friends in Washington, but it wasn't the same. They were social friends not soul mates.

No history there.

History meant you didn't have to explain. That you could start up right where you left off.

With history, the chaff had already been separated from the wheat. Accepting each other as you were. Being loved in spite of yourself.

She thought of Daniel but resisted the urge to lift her gaze. He'd had to overlook so much in her.

Regardless of what had happened in the war that had so changed her feelings for him, she'd seen his innate goodness during these shared days that made her remember why she had once loved him.

Daisy stroked her hand. "It's been a long day. How are you holding up?"

"I'm fine. A bit tired."

"I hate leaving you alone tonight," Daisy said.

"I'm not alone. Helen's staying." She smiled at the woman who had become one of her dear friends.

"Of course," Daisy said. "I'd forgotten."

Claire sighed. "I guess tomorrow I'll have to start going through Mother's things. Helen said she'd help. But still, it's daunting. Mother was such a collector. . .and—"

"You can count on me, too. You know that," Daisy said.

Claire felt the sadness welling up inside her. "It's. . .hard."

Daniel stood up and pulled a large handkerchief from his pocket and handed it to her. "Don't worry, it's clean." He smiled. "I saved it for just such a moment."

"Always the Boy Scout," Jack mumbled, leaning back in his chair and closing his eyes.

"Don't make fun of Daniel," Daisy said. "He really is a

Boy Scout, the way he takes up lost causes."

"Here, here," Helen said, cocking her elbow on the arm of the couch and resting her forehead in her hand.

"Daniel also helped us save Lou's garage." Daisy turned to Claire. "She's the old lady with property next to the church the bank was going to foreclose on."

"I can't take credit there, Daisy. You and Jack were responsible for that." Daniel stretched out his legs and crossed his ankles

"Mainly my wife," Jack muttered.

"But you did all the legal work for free," Daisy reminded Daniel.

"All these accolades just for handing a lady a handkerchief." Daniel suppressed a smile.

Claire's gaze rested on her clasped hands. "You've all been so wonderful. I don't know how I could have gotten through it without you. . . . You've been like family."

"I am family," Daisy said, reaching over and squeezing her hand. "Two orphans who have adopted each other."

Claire returned a grateful smile.

"I hope you're going to stay," Daisy said. "This is your home. This is where your heart is."

"I'll stay for a while. I still have my assignment for *Life*. And of course, there's the estate to settle." She glanced at Daniel. "I'll have to sell the house."

"You don't have to."

"My life's in Washington now. My career."

"But you travel wherever your story takes you," Daisy said. "Couldn't this be your home base?" She dropped her head on Claire's shoulder. "Now that you've come home, I don't want to lose you again. Do we, Jack?"

"Claire has to do what will make her happy," Daniel said.

The trouble was that Claire was beginning to wonder what would make her happy.

Helen, who'd been sitting quietly, said, "What do they say? You should wait a year before making any major decisions."

"Unless you don't want to lose your job," Claire said.

"Helen's right," Daisy said. "Even if you go back to Washington, you can keep the house. You can always lease it if you need the money. Isn't that right, Daniel?"

"It is. But I doubt money will be an issue," Daniel said.

Claire directed her words to Daisy. "It sounds as if you have my future all worked out."

"What's new?" Jack mumbled, his eyes still closed.

"Like I said," Helen interjected, "in a year—"

"Listen to Helen. She's the practical one." Daisy put her head on Claire's shoulder again. "Besides, I need you to baby-sit."

Jack's eyes popped open. "I thought that was our secret."

"Well, it was," Daisy said, "but this just seemed like a good time to tell it." Suddenly, she looked worried. "Oh, I hope it was. It almost seemed. . .oh, I don't know, part of God's plan."

A baby. Claire threw her arms around her friend. "Oh, Daisy, I couldn't be more thrilled." She laughed past her tears. "God's timing is perfect."

"I had something to do with it," Jack grumbled good-naturedly.

"Don't cry," Daisy said, brushing the wetness from Claire's cheeks with her hand.

Claire sniffed.

"It's only been two months," Daisy said proudly, "and I'm already beginning to show."

Helen leaned over and studied their petite friend.

"Where, on your fingernails?"

Daisy made a face and tried, without much success, to puff out her stomach.

She looked at Claire. "So, you see, I'm going to need all the help I can get decorating the baby's room, buying things—"

"Come now, Daisy," Jack said, "of all people, you are the last person who needs help to spend money."

"But it's more fun with a friend," Daisy said. She leaned over and looked at Helen. "You'll come, too, Helen."

"Daisy forgets that it's not good form for a minister to spend extravagantly."

Daisy shrugged. "That's what you get for marrying into money." She looked fondly at her husband. "Tell them the name we've picked if it's a girl."

Jack lowered his feet from the footstool and sat upright in his chair. He looked at Claire. "If it's all right with you," he said quietly, "we thought we'd name her Ruth, after your mother."

"Why. . .why I think that's wonderful," Claire said.

She'd said it, and she meant it. Part of her, at least. There was a time when she'd wanted to name her own daughter Ruth if she'd had a girl. Back when she thought she'd have children of her own. Before. . .

For a moment she felt a deeper sadness, mourning not only the loss of her mother but the children she might never have.

twenty-two

Daniel's hand rested on the file containing the documents of Ruth's estate. As her attorney and executor, he knew that the probate procedure was the easy part. Claire, as Ruth's only heir, would be financially secure.

Fulfilling his promise to Ruth was the real challenge.

Since the funeral, he'd come to realize how much he still cared for Claire. Far more than he wanted to.

During these past weeks—Ruth's final days, her death, the funeral—he'd become aware of how vulnerable and alone Claire truly was.

For his own sake, he couldn't allow his natural protective instincts toward her to become a love deeper than that of a concerned friend.

He picked up the phone and dialed her number.

Claire answered on the third ring.

"Hello, Claire, it's Daniel."

"I recognized your voice."

"How are you doing?"

"I'm all right." She sounded disconsolate. "I just wish it would stop raining."

"I know what you mean. But it will eventually. It always does."

"If I didn't know you better, I'd think you were dispensing one of those meaningless metaphors for grieving. Time will heal—"

"Fortunately, you know me better."

She began to cry. "I guess the reality is beginning to set

in. I'm never going to. . .to see her again. At least not for a long time. . . Not until I. . ."

Daniel cradled the phone, listening to her quiet weeping. All he could think to say was, "I'm sorry."

She sniffled and sighed. "I know you are. Believe it or not, hearing you say it helps."

"I'm glad." He smiled.

She blew her nose. "It's funny, I was just about to call you."

"Now you can save your nickel," Daniel said, shifting his elbow to the arm of his desk chair.

Sighing, she said, "I think I need a break, Daniel. I've been cooped up in this house so long, I feel as if I can't breathe." Her voice caught. "Not that I resent it. I wouldn't have traded the time with Mother for anything. But now I'm faced with having to sort through her things and make decisions, and I just. . .I can't. I'm just not ready to face it."

"That doesn't surprise me. There's no rush, Claire."

"Helen and I were talking. I thought maybe I could get started on my *Life* assignment."

"Good idea."

"She talked to her family about my interviewing them. It took some persuasion."

"They're very private people," Daniel said.

"I know. But I think she convinced them. We wanted to discuss it with you before we set a time. They know you and respect you—"

"You want me to come along?" The thought pleased him. Watching Claire work would be an interesting experience.

"Would you? We both think they would be more comfortable if you were there."

"Of course." As they talked, he pictured Claire sitting at the desk. He wondered what she was wearing. Was her hair hanging loose around her face, or had she pulled it back into a bun? "But it has to be in the evening or on a Saturday. I'm pretty well booked during the day for the next couple of weeks."

"I'm sure we can work out a time."

"I'm glad they're willing." He loved the shine and the silky texture of her hair when she wore it down. "They're good people. I think you'll like them."

"I hope they'll like me."

"That doesn't sound like the confident girl I once knew," he said gently.

"I don't feel like the confident girl you once knew. But like the rain, this, too, will pass."

"Claire."

"Yes?"

"You're going to be fine."

Silence suspended between them.

"I know," Claire finally said, her voice hardly above a whisper.

He wished he were there to hold her and comfort her.

&

As arranged, two days later, on a brisk but blessedly sunny Saturday afternoon, Daniel and Claire strode up the front walk of a dilapidated apartment house in a poor section of Los Angeles. He carried Claire's tape recorder. She had slung her bulky camera equipment across her shoulder.

Three Oriental boys were playing kick ball in the street behind them, and as they mounted the steps, a gaggle of little Japanese girls leaning against the rail of the apartment next door twittered and whispered behind their hands.

Claire paused.

Daniel could see the tension in the set of her lips and the

hesitation in her eyes.

"You're going to do fine," he said.

"I'm not worried about how I'm going to do." She turned toward him. "I'm worried about how I'm suddenly beginning to feel. Aside from Helen, I've had next to no contact with Japanese people. As a race, I've thought of them only as my brother's killers." A panicked look flashed across her face. "Suddenly, I'm wondering what I'm doing here. I feel so torn."

It was his fault. He should have discouraged her when she called. This was too much for her to have taken on so soon after her mother's passing, particularly when she carried so many painful memories over her brother's death.

But it was too late to change course now. Helen was expecting them.

She must have heard them. The door opened, and there she was, greeting them warmly as she ushered them into a small, spotless, sparsely furnished, one-bedroom apartment.

Five people called it home.

The family, already gathered in the living room, rose, greeting Daniel as he and Claire entered. For Claire, their smiles held a certain reserve, a veiled resistance.

An elderly Japanese lady and gentleman, standing side by side in front of the beige couch, bowed slightly as Helen introduced them. "My parents, Aki and Chiyo Yamashida. You remember Daniel." She took Claire's hand. "And this is my friend, Claire, whom I told you about."

Claire shifted her camera case and bowed. "*Doozo yoroshiku.*"

Daniel turned and stared at her.

"Helen taught me," she murmured.

The greeting seemed to tickle Helen's parents, and they

smiled as they bowed in response. *"Doozo yoroshiku."*

"Nice to meet you," Helen translated for Daniel, grinning.

Daniel was impressed. Clever girl. Claire had been worried that they might not like her, and already she had them in the palm of her hand.

"This is my brother, Paul," Helen said, drawing Claire toward a well-built young man, handsome, and tall for a Japanese. He stood by a scarred dining table at the end of the room, leaning on a crutch. An empty trouser leg was folded and pinned up at his left knee.

"Helen's explained to us about the article you're doing," he said. "The story needs to be told."

Claire grasped his outstretched hand in both of hers. "Thank you and your family, Paul, for giving me the opportunity to tell it."

She wasn't just clever, Daniel thought, she was kind. With her sincerity and honest interest, he could see any vestiges of Paul's reticence dissolve. He sensed the others in the room understood, as he did, that she had not come to exploit their story but to share it.

"And this is my Sara." Helen dropped her arm around the shoulders of a young girl about nine or ten with a round face and dancing black eyes beneath straight, dark bangs.

The child returned a shy smile.

Daniel and Claire had talked about Sara on the drive over. She had lived in Children's Village, the Manzanar orphanage, along with a hundred others, some as young as six months.

"Certainly a threat to American security," Claire had observed dryly, then asked, "What was the orphanage like?"

"A relatively happy place, I understand." He'd told her about the separate barracks for the boys and one for the girls and how they ate their meals in their own mess hall but schooled with the other camp children.

Helen had been Sara's teacher. When the camp was disbanded, she couldn't stand the idea of Sara going to some foster home.

"So she adopted her. And you were the lawyer in the adoption." That part of the story Helen had already told Claire.

Looking at the shy, sweet-faced child, Daniel felt a surge of pride that he had been able to help find her a home where she would be loved and cherished the way all children deserve.

In the bedroom doorway, a sturdy, sad-looking young woman with downcast eyes suddenly appeared.

"Fumiko, you decided to join us." Helen turned to Claire. "This is my cousin Fumiko. Daniel, I don't believe you've met her, either. Fumiko isn't sure she wants to participate. But I told her to join us anyway and she could decide."

Although Daniel and Fumiko hadn't previously met, Helen had told him her story. Sadly, it was not an isolated one.

Her father and mother had immigrated to America in the twenties. Their children were born here and were citizens. Her father had been a successful businessman and a respected community leader. After Pearl Harbor, he lost everything he valued, including his self-respect. When the family reached the camp, he committed suicide.

Daniel knew Fumiko was younger than Helen, but she looked years older. Her face was lined with an indelible sadness.

Hers was one story Daniel doubted Claire would get.

"Please sit down," Helen said. "I've prepared tea."

Fumiko slipped silently into the room, pulling one of the chairs from the dining table into the farthest corner.

Sara leaned against Paul, who had lowered himself into his chair by the table. Daniel, after making room for the tape recorder on the coffee table and plugging it into a nearby outlet, sat down next to Helen's father.

"Does anyone object if I tape this?" Claire asked, dropping into the chair next to the couch.

"I already told them you would," Helen said, carrying in a tray of tea and sweets and putting them on the coffee table beside the tape recorder. She poured each of them a cup, passed the treats, and pulled a chair from the dining table, placing it next to Claire.

Claire took a sip of tea and set down her cup. "I'm going to pretty much let you all have free rein. I may prompt you with a question to keep you on track, but I want you to feel free to say anything that comes into your head. . .or your heart." She smiled. "From time to time, I'll be shooting some pictures. But don't worry, you'll have a chance to approve everything that goes into the article before I submit it to my editor. Do you have any questions?" She looked around the room. "Then let's turn on the tape recorder."

twenty-three

Daniel pressed down the button to start the tape recorder.

"Where were you all when you received the news of Pearl Harbor?" Claire asked, removing her camera from its case.

Paul answered. "The family was ready to go to the late service at church. I was running behind because I'd been fooling around with my ham radio. I remember Chichi—Dad—and I had a big argument." He gave his father a wry smile. "I left the radio on while I got dressed and heard the announcement."

"So you told the family."

Paul nodded.

Claire pressed gently. "What was their reaction?"

Paul frowned. "What you'd expect. Shock, disbelief." He looked again at his father, his expression sad. "I remember it was the first time I ever saw Chichi cry."

His father, Aki, lowered his head, and Chiyo, who had been sitting quietly beside her husband, reached over and covered his hand with hers.

It was a touching gesture that Daniel noticed Claire caught on camera.

"Those were bad days," Helen said. "We'd known plenty of prejudice before, but nothing like after Pearl Harbor. And then two months later, in February, President Roosevelt signed the executive order that resulted in the evacuation."

Aki shook his head, his accent thickening with sadness. "Forty-eight hours to choose from lifetime. We pack only

128

what we able to carry."

"I remember how sad I felt having to leave my dog, Lucy," Helen said. "She was an old dog. I'd had her since I was twelve, and I knew I'd probably never see her again. She'd most likely be dead before we got out." She looked at her brother. "Remember, Paul, the folks next door said they'd take care of her?"

Sara moved over and sat down on the floor next to Helen's chair. Resting her head against Helen's knee, she looked up at her adopted mother with sympathy shimmering in her liquid black eyes.

Claire snapped that picture, too.

"Some friends *they* turned out to be," Paul snorted, his face darkening. "Chichi knew we would lose the house if he couldn't make the mortgage payments. Our *friend* next door said he'd see that it was rented and make the payments for us. He rented it all right but kept the money, let it be foreclosed, and bought it himself."

"At least he was nice to the dog," Helen said dryly.

"That's how Helen and I met," Daniel said to Claire. "When she came to me about a lawsuit."

"You had a business, didn't you, Mr. Yamashida?" Claire asked, snapping a close-up of him.

Aki's eyes misted as he described locking up his produce store for the last time. He shook his head as if he still found it hard to believe.

Daniel looked over at Claire. He'd assumed she was waiting for Aki to collect his thoughts, but it was obvious from her distressed expression, she was using the time to collect her own.

She may be a professional, he thought, *but objective she is not.* Her feelings were eloquently written on her expressive face.

When she spoke, her voice was husky but controlled. "Then you were sent to the internment camp at Manzanar."

"No," Helen answered. "They bussed us first to Santa Anita Race Track to wait for our permanent assignments. Hundreds of us housed in horse stalls. They'd cleaned them, but they still stank of straw and manure. . . . The latrines weren't much better." Her tone was bitter.

"Were you with the family then?" Claire asked Paul.

Paul nodded. "Then I enlisted. When they were being transferred to Manzanar, I was being inducted into the army at Fort MacArthur in San Pedro."

"I want to get back to that," Claire said, "but first let me hear about Manzanar." She turned to Helen.

"Tell Claire what you remember the first time you saw the camp, Chichi," Helen said to her father.

Aki paused, reflecting. "I remember cold. Bitter cold and wind." He raised his eyes. "Guard towers, barbed wire, rows of barracks. I remember waking first morning and seeing my head outlined in layer of sand on mattress. Sand blown in through cracks in floor."

"Those straw mattresses were something else," Helen mused. "But you got used to them."

"Scorpions. Don't forget scorpions," Chiyo said in her small voice.

"I remember them." Sara bounced onto her knees. "We used to catch them in jars."

"And hot in summer," Chiyo added.

"That's putting it mildly," Helen said. "Bitter cold as the winters were, the searing summer sun beating down on those barracks was stifling."

"Tell me about living in the barracks," Claire said, focusing her camera on Helen.

"Well, there were several families to a barracks. We'd put a sheet between us for privacy." She looked over at her mother. "I remember how you would cry at night."

Her mother's eyes grew moist. "I not think you hear me."

"Everybody heard you. We couldn't help it."

"Oh, my." Chiyo covered her face.

Aki flashed his daughter a warning look. "No worry, Chiyo. Nobody hear. They too busy crying, too."

"It was harder on the older generation like my parents," Helen said. "Communal latrines." She shuddered. "No privacy. Lining up to eat in the mess hall. So many things. It was as if we'd lost our identity."

Daniel saw Claire touch Helen's shoulder.

"Parents couldn't discipline their children in the same way. Kids didn't pay attention. Didn't give respect to their elders, which is strong in the Japanese culture. It was like summer camp all year round."

"Not in winter," Sara said, wrapping her arms around herself and pretending to shiver.

Helen stroked her hair and smiled. "I was speaking metaphorically, dear. You remember that word from vocabulary."

"One thing that represents another," Sara quoted.

"Smart girl."

"But still, we make best of it," Aki said. "We make a life. Babies born. People die. We have school and hospital and newspaper. I plant my garden."

"We go to church," Chiyo said.

Throughout the conversation, Fumiko sat silent in the corner, as if she'd just faded into the striped beige wallpaper. Daniel had actually forgotten about her, and so, it seemed, had the rest of the family. He wondered if that was the way it always was.

Claire glanced at her watch. "Now is a good time to take a break while I change the tape in the recorder. Then I'd like to hear about Paul's experience in the army."

"I'll make more tea," Helen said. "Is there a helper nearby?"

"Me." Sara jumped up and followed her into the kitchen.

The postage-stamp kitchen was open to the living room, and Daniel could see them busying themselves—Helen putting on the kettle, Sara replenishing the cookie plate.

He watched Claire massage the back of her neck and stand up, smoothing the forest green skirt over her slim hips, adjusting the collar of her blouse over the matching sweater. Even in this tailored ensemble, she had a femininity that he found enormously appealing.

She looked down at him.

In her eyes he read a concern and compassion that reminded him of years past when just a glance, a touch conveyed all they needed to communicate.

While Helen refreshed their tea and Sara passed cookies, Claire snapped the rest of her photos. She even caught Fumiko in an unguarded moment.

Returning the camera to its case, she flipped on the tape recorder, then focused on Paul. "You volunteered."

Paul nodded. "My friends and I. We wanted to prove that we were good Americans. Loyal to our country."

"And you were in the 442nd Regimental Combat Team."

"As Japanese, it was our only choice." He glanced back at Fumiko. "Fumiko's brother was a chaplain."

"Was he?" Claire looked over at Fumiko, who nodded in response.

Daniel had the feeling that no amount of waiting would get more than that from her.

"As I understand it, that team along with the 100th

Infantry Battalion were the most decorated combat units for size and for length of service in U.S. military history."

"Yeah." Paul shifted in his chair. "Ironic, isn't it? While we're fighting for our country, our country throws our families in prison."

"Relocation centers," Aki murmured.

"Internment camps," Helen muttered.

"What's the difference? There was a fence too high to climb, and the guns were pointed inward," Paul said, his voice harsh.

For a minute, everyone was silent.

Claire cleared her throat. "Tell me about the army, Paul."

"We had the same training as every other soldier. Good enough to send us forward into the thick of things. You've heard of Sergeant Ted Tanouye."

Claire looked blank.

"I certainly have," Daniel said.

"Bravest man I've ever known. I had the privilege of serving under him."

Claire leaned forward. "Tell us about him."

"He wasn't like other sergeants. He had patience, and he tried to explain things to his men instead of just giving orders.

"We'd been pinned down for two days by machine-gun fire. Given up hope. We didn't have a chance. But Ted wouldn't accept that. His mission was to protect his men, even at the expense of his own life.

"He crawled forward alone and wiped out the first nest of Germans. The second opened fire on him, and he out-gunned them, too. We couldn't believe it. Even after he was wounded in his arm by a grenade, he kept on going until he'd cleaned out all six nests. Single-handedly."

"He sounds superhuman." Claire's voice expressed awe.

"We thought so." Paul shook his head.

A look of pain came into his eyes. "When he recovered, he rejoined the unit. We were on the Arno River." Paul sighed. "I was standing near him when it happened. He was crouched down inspecting a German land mine when another soldier accidentally stepped on the attached trip wire. I can still hear the sound, feel the blast. The sergeant took the brunt. If it weren't for Ted, I wouldn't be alive."

Daniel glanced around the still room. It was as if their collective breath were suspended, waiting.

Paul continued, his voice rough with emotion. "As they carried Ted off the field, he lived long enough to shout our battalion motto. 'Go for broke!' "

"Go for broke." Paul's voice fell to a whisper. "He took care of his men. Most of us were only eighteen or nineteen. Ted was twenty-four." He dropped his head into his hands.

Daniel turned away. He couldn't bear to watch the anguish in Paul's shaking shoulders and silent sobs. He glanced over at Claire and saw tears coursing down her cheeks.

The voices of the boys outside playing kick ball, a passing car cut the silence as Paul struggled to get himself under control.

When he finally lifted his head, his face was ravaged with grief and with rage. "If he'd been white, they'd have given him the Medal of Honor."

twenty-four

Dark had overtaken the daylight by the time Claire and Daniel left the Yamashida apartment. Helen had invited them to stay for dinner. Although Claire knew the invitation was sincere, she suspected it was nevertheless out of courtesy. She, for one, was too emotionally drained to even think of food, and she couldn't believe that the Yamashida family didn't feel the same.

Daniel insisted on carrying her camera and tape recorder. In spite of the bulky equipment, he still managed to take her elbow and guide her down the front steps.

Lights glowed in the curtained windows of adjacent apartments. The murmur of voices and the aroma of barbecue wafted on the chill air.

"I thought barbecuing was a summer sport," Daniel mused, opening the car door and securing her equipment before helping her in on the passenger side.

Claire looked up at the Yamashida apartment.

It was still dark.

She tried to keep back the tears, but it was a futile effort.

How professional was this?

She'd seen sad things, the aftermath of brutality both in body and spirit. But she'd never reacted like this before. Never been so emotionally involved. In the few hours she'd spent with Helen and her family, she had lost herself in their suffering.

She felt the sad acceptance of Aki and Chiyo, Paul's bone-deep bitterness.

135

Who could blame him?

And dear Helen, strong and persistent despite it all.

What started as a trickle turned into a torrent. She leaned against the car door and sobbed.

She sobbed for her mother and for her brother. But most of all she sobbed for this luckless family that had been buffeted by prejudice and their country's betrayal.

She felt Daniel's hand on her shoulder, a gentle reminder of the one comforting source of strength she had left.

Despite everything that had separated them in the past, no matter what the future held, she knew with all her heart that Daniel would always be there if she needed him. She was grateful that, as always, he had the wisdom to keep silent while her emotional roller coaster ran its course.

He handed her his handkerchief.

"I know. It's clean," she said, wiping her eyes and blowing her nose. "It seems like you always carry a spare."

"Only when I'm with you."

"I didn't know I was such a crybaby."

"You have reason." He turned the key in the ignition, shifted into gear, and wheeled out onto the empty street.

"How could they have survived with the whole world abusing them?" she said.

"I suspect it was their faith."

"That sounds so pat." She glanced at him. "Faith in a God who would let all that happen to them?"

"Come on, Claire. You know better than that." It was the first time since her return that he'd used anything but a conciliatory tone with her. "It's not God. It's man." Impatiently, Daniel shifted gears. "God helps us get through the things that we do to each other. . .or to ourselves," he muttered.

In a gentler voice, he quoted, " 'If it had not been the

Lord who was on our side, when men rose up against us: Then they had swallowed us up. . . .' "

"From Psalms?"

He nodded. "One twenty-four."

"You missed your calling, Daniel," Claire said dryly. "You should have been a preacher."

"I know you mean that as a compliment."

"By all means."

"The verse ends," he continued, apparently intent on proving her right, " 'Our soul is escaped as a bird out of the snare of the fowlers; the snare is broken, and we are escaped. Our help is in the name of the Lord.' In other words—"

"If our soul is free, then so are we."

"You got it."

"Tell that to Paul." Claire sniffed and blew her nose again.

Daniel looked somber. "I wish I could." His voice sounded tired and sad. "There's a lot I don't know the answers to, Claire, that's for sure." His smile was grim. "I don't even know most of the questions." Braking for a stoplight, he looked over at her. "I guess that's where faith begins."

She had always grappled with a faith in which Daniel had seemed so secure. It was a relief to know that he had his doubts, too.

Doubts were such a lonely battle.

They were silent for a time. Long enough for Claire to get her emotions back in check.

"I can't believe that I knew so little about this Japanese situation," she murmured.

"You're not alone. Few people do."

"There were so many of them. How many—120,000 in the camps? Unbelievable."

Daniel nodded.

"Where did they go when they were set free? Most of them had lost their homes, their jobs. Nobody wants to hire them. What happens to them now? What happens to men like Paul?"

Daniel shook his head. "All we can do is keep trying to help them."

"It doesn't seem as if there are enough people like you willing to do that."

"There are some out there. Don't forget Daisy and Jack and the other folks at Good Shepherd Community like Mrs. Beemer and Miss Parrott."

"That's true. But I'm afraid the majority of Americans don't care."

"Or don't know. I think if more people knew. . ." Daniel glanced at her. "That's why this article you're doing is so important."

"I hope so."

Claire stared out the window at the headlights of oncoming cars as they drove on in silence. Finally, she said quietly, "I needed to do this for myself, too, Daniel. I think my editor, Larry, realized that when he gave me the assignment."

She tightened the belt of her jacket. "I was so miserable and angry when I came back from Washington. I hated everything Japanese. Even the antique imported chest in my mother's living room. I was so transfixed with my own pain that I didn't notice other people's suffering."

"Don't be so hard on yourself," Daniel said, making a left onto Claire's street. "They say there's a process to grieving. Takes time." He pulled into her driveway and cut the engine.

She turned to him. "This afternoon, I saw not just with my head but with my heart. Helen and Paul and little Sara are as American as I am. I needed to hear their stories. I needed to understand so I could lay the anguish of Billy's death to rest."

She leaned back against the car door. She could barely make out his features from the clock light on the dashboard. In a quiet voice, she said, "You've been very patient with me."

"Claire—"

"No, I mean it. And I'm grateful."

"You would have done the same for me," he said.

"I don't think so." She breathed a regretful sigh. "No," she sighed, "I don't think I would have."

After a pause, he asked, "Would you now?"

He was facing her, leaning back against the car door on his side. They were about as far apart physically as the interior of the car would allow, yet there was an invisible pull between them.

"Honestly?" she asked.

Suddenly, he laughed, breaking the string of tension. "On second thought, not if it's going to hurt my feelings."

"You're tougher than that," she said lightly.

"I hope so."

"I'll answer your question." She turned serious. "I hope I would be as kind. Certainly there's a better chance now than when I first arrived." She let a smile seep into her tone. "But please, don't put me to the test." Abruptly, she turned and opened the door. "I've got to go in."

Daniel got out and walked over to her side of the car, reaching into the backseat for her camera and tape recorder.

As she fumbled in her purse at the front door for her key, she glanced back at him. "Do you want to come in for a sandwich or something?"

"I thought you weren't hungry."

"I'm not. But you might be. I can't promise anything fancy. I don't know what Helen left in the refrigerator."

She couldn't make out his expression in the dark. But she could sense the thoughts processing through his brain: Should he? Shouldn't he? Would it be starting something he didn't want to deal with again?

"Oh, come on, Daniel. It's just a sandwich. I'm not offering a full-course meal. You won't be obligated."

She hoped he'd take her up on it, see the invitation as she'd intended, a chance to prove that, despite their differences, she wanted to be his friend again.

twenty-five

"Unless, of course, you have other plans for dinner," Claire said nonchalantly as she pushed open her front door.

"No plans," Daniel said.

"Well, then?"

"Why not?"

He put the camera case and tape recorder on the floor by the table in the entry and followed Claire into the den.

She kicked off her heels and dropped her jacket over the back of the chair flanking the fireplace, then padded across the carpet to the kitchen. She peered into the refrigerator. "Not much of interest, I'm afraid." She glanced over her shoulder at him. "I hope you're not very hungry."

"Whatever."

"Ah. Wait just a minute. I've struck gold." She pulled out a jar of peanut butter and a loaf of whole wheat bread. "Grilled peanut butter sandwiches."

"My favorite." Daniel grinned. "You remembered."

"How could I forget?"

"That was one passion we shared." He smiled.

Among others, she thought with a sigh. "You light the fire."

As the sandwiches grilled, Claire set a tray for each of them. Along with half a banana, she dropped a handful of potato chips on both plates and poured two glasses of milk.

She flipped the sandwiches, cut them crosswise into triangles, and slid them onto the plates.

"I thought you weren't hungry," Daniel said, eyeing the trays.

"When the peanut butter started to melt, my stomach told me otherwise." She handed him a tray. "There was only one banana. Sorry, we have to share."

"It won't be the first time." He held his tray and added quietly, "Nor the last, I hope."

He'd gotten her message.

It wasn't relief exactly that she felt. More a sense of peace that maybe a fence had been mended. No need to discuss the breech. Just start from now. It was enough to know that he had recognized and accepted her gesture of friendship.

They set their trays on the coffee table in front of the couch, chewing companionably and gazing into the fire. Not saying much other than a satisfied "mmm" from time to time.

Daniel wiped his mouth and sat back. "I had forgotten what a great cook you were."

"Yes, well this is about as good as it gets, if you recall." Claire popped the final potato chip into her mouth.

His arm was over the back of the couch, his hand inches from her shoulder.

Still, it made her slightly uncomfortable. She adjusted a pillow behind her and slipped deftly just out of reach into the corner, tucking her knees up under her. "You were the one who could cook. Do you still?"

"One of these days, I'll give you a chance to find out. If you play your cards right."

"I told you this sumptuous repast did not obligate you to reciprocate."

"I realize that." His eyes took on a lazy look. "But it would be fun to exercise my culinary skills for someone with such refined and sophisticated taste."

Claire snuggled down deeper into the corner of the couch, warmed by the fire and the bantering exchange.

"Have you given any thought to what your plans are?" Daniel asked.

She nodded. "For one thing, I'm not going to sell the house for a while."

"Then you'll be staying."

"No."

The pleased look that had stamped his face disappeared.

"I thought I'd lease it. I've decided to go back to Washington." She picked at a thread in the couch fabric. "Too many sad memories here."

"I hope I'm not one of them," Daniel said quietly, crossing his arms and giving her a direct look.

He was, and he wasn't.

Intuiting her thoughts, he said, "Don't worry, Claire. You'll have no problems from this quarter. You're safe with me."

Was she?

"As safe as you want to be."

That was the wrinkle. She wanted to be his friend but feared where too much proximity might lead.

"Going back to Washington will give me the perspective I need. Wasn't it Helen who said no serious decisions should be made for a year?"

"Good advice." He gazed into the fire for several minutes then turned back to her. "When do you think you'll leave?"

"It won't be for a while. If I lease the house, I'll have to go through Mother's things. Decide what to keep and what to put into storage."

"And you still have the article to write."

"I can do that in Washington. I might want to do a couple more interviews, maybe attend another meeting or two. But the rest of the research I can do back there."

"I thought you said you were going to let Helen and the

family sign off on the article before you gave it to your editor."

"I did, and I will. Moving back there doesn't preclude a visit home. In fact, the magazine will probably pay for it."

"I'm glad to hear you still call this home," he murmured.

"Habit." She shrugged then smiled. "Anyway, it's hard to get rid of a bad penny like me."

"Did you hear me say I wanted to?" he asked lightly.

With a nervous laugh, Claire pulled her gaze from his. "Probably only because you're too kind."

She leaned forward and began to stack the trays.

"Let me do that."

"No, no. You're the guest."

Still he reached out, and his hand brushed hers.

Such a small gesture for such an electric response.

They both froze.

Claire's breath caught.

She could see his eyes narrow, calculating, trying to decide.

Slowly he pulled back.

The moment passed, but she knew it was not lost to either of them. She picked up the stacked trays and carried them into the kitchen.

A few minutes later, she accompanied him out onto the front porch to say good night.

The air was cold. She shivered, wrapping her arms around herself for warmth.

Daniel stood on the step below, his face level with hers. The porch light was on, and while she remained in the shadows, every nuance of his expression was clear to her.

"It's been an amazing day. One I will never forget," she said.

His gaze scanned her face. "Amazing."

In more ways—she was sure—than either of them had anticipated.

"Thank you for letting me share it with you," he said quietly.

Then in a gesture that was at once bold and gentle, he leaned forward and kissed her on the lips. A whisper of a kiss. Light and lingering.

She allowed it.

She didn't turn away or protest.

Then he was gone.

She stood, watching until the back lights of his car disappeared, her mouth still tingling with the gentle ardor of his kiss.

twenty-six

This wasn't turning out at all the way she'd expected or intended.

That kiss had been the catalyst for an eruption of feelings that, until the night before, Claire had managed to successfully submerge.

And it wasn't even much of a kiss as kisses go. Their lips had barely touched. Yet it had held a promise and passion that even now, in remembering, took her breath away.

She'd always given Daniel credit for a number of sterling qualities. But it had also occurred to her that he'd polished those qualities partially out of a sense of guilt.

It didn't lessen the good he did, only the motive behind the deeds.

Should that matter?

Regardless of how she felt about him, the fundamental issue was the same. Daniel Essex was a coward who in a time of war had betrayed his country and his friends.

Even if he was never tested again, could she respect him for his goodness and ignore that crucial flaw?

She'd changed her attitude toward the Japanese. Could she do the same toward Daniel?

She honestly didn't know.

And even if her attitude did soften, she wondered if it actually mattered.

Did he really care about her as much as he seemed to? Or was it just her latent feelings for him coming to the surface?

Over their morning coffee, she and Helen had talked about the remarkable afternoon Claire had spent with Helen's family. How open they had been, how brave and generous in sharing their story.

She thought especially of Paul's courage and sacrifice in putting his life on the line for a country that had betrayed and vilified him and his people.

The comparison between Paul and Daniel made Daniel's position as a conscientious objector even more odious.

How could he look a man like Paul Yamashida in the face?

This was the turmoil of her thoughts as she and Helen began the task of sorting through and packing up her mother's effects.

While Helen started boxing the extensive collection of fine china, Claire began going through her mother's personal possessions.

A sad and difficult task.

Her mother had not only been a collector of lovely antiques and artifacts, but she was a sentimental collector who had saved her husband's love letters, her children's drawings and notes, and a ceramic seal that Claire had sculpted in third grade. She had saved report cards and nosegays her children had made for her on Easters throughout the years, each dried and separately wrapped in tissue. Claire was sure that not a homemade Christmas, birthday, or holiday card was missing since she and Billy had started scribbling on foolscap in the nursery at church.

As she shuffled through the boxes, she was swamped with happy memories that brought, with the smiles, the poignant tears of loss.

It wasn't long into this journey that she came upon the box containing Billy's letters, every one of them from boot camp to the day before he died.

She sat on her mother's bed, the contents of the box spread around her. As she turned the thin, tissuelike airmail paper, she was reminded of her brother's sense of humor as he described in hilarious detail their K rations, the idiosyncrasies of his fellow soldiers, the heat and the flies, and the colonel's "one holer"—the latrine he'd been ordered to build in the heat of battle so that their commanding officer could have some privacy.

Always upbeat. Always optimistic.

Always ending "Not to worry, Mom, I say my prayers every night."

But there was one letter that was different. It read as if he might have known it was his last:

> . . . *Daniel and I talked a lot about what we would do if we were called up. We wondered how either of us could kill another human being, our faith being what it is.*
>
> *Now I know.*
>
> *I didn't think I could, but I have. There are a lot of things you do when you have to.*
>
> *It's not that I'm not proud to be here fighting. This is a just war against a ruthless tyranny. But the truth is, it wasn't an easy decision, even though I knew you and Sis would support me whatever I did.*
>
> *I've often wondered, though, had I felt as strongly as Daniel, would I have had his courage? Would I have been willing to be scorned and ostracized as he's been?*
>
> *Daniel's a brave man. I don't want you to forget it. He stood up for what he thought was right despite what other people would say. And don't think he hasn't paid the price. He's been beaten up and spit on. Once a guy even*

tried to run him over.

One of the signs I saw in a restaurant window: "No skunks allowed, so you conscientious objectors keep the h—— out."

And that was a mild one.

Daniel's as patriotic an American as I am, Mom, but he's a Christian first, who takes "thou shalt not kill" very seriously.

He needs to know that we understand and support him.

If I don't get the chance to tell him, I'm counting on you. I've never felt other than honored to be his friend and proud of him for having the guts to make the decision he did, to go against the tide.

We lost track soon after I was inducted. I'm worried that they've put him in prison. But I know wherever he is, he'll be doing the Lord's work.

Well, the light's almost gone. Not to worry, Mom, I'm saying my prayers.

> *Love,*
> *Your son, Bill*

Billy had also struggled with his decision to serve his country.

Claire never knew that. Obviously, until the end, neither had her mother.

He and Daniel had wrestled with a basic tenet of their faith, "Thou shalt not kill." Each had chosen his own path.

The handwritten words of the letter shimmered through the watery lenses of Claire's eyes. She squeezed them shut, determined not to give in to the tears that lately so often flowed.

Neither her beloved brother nor the man she loved had trusted her enough to share their battle with her.

Did they want to spare her as men so often think they should?

Or did they think that she would not understand?

If they had confided in her, if she had been able to see the torment and sincerity of their struggle, she would have realized then what it had taken until now to comprehend.

They had denied her that opportunity.

An overwhelming sense of failure and loss fell over her, as well as a feeling of betrayal at their lack of trust. At Daniel's lack of trust.

She smoothed the creased pages of Billy's letter and read again, "I knew you and Sis would support me whatever my decision. . . ."

No doubt Daniel had had the same expectation.

But Billy would have explained his reasons.

Not Daniel.

He'd expected her to intuit his thoughts, to automatically accept such a life-altering decision. He'd chosen not to share his struggle with her, the woman who would be most affected by that decision. The woman with whom he expected to spend his life.

She had loved him madly, desperately. He had been her hero even before he was her love. She'd looked up to him as a man of ultimate courage and faith.

She'd been so proud that he had chosen her.

So when he took his silent path, her devastation, her disillusionment had been overwhelming.

She knew what conscientious objectors were. "They had a yellow streak running down their backs," as one newspaper so aptly put it.

She had turned her back on him.

When Billy had honorably answered his call to go, then died, as far as she was concerned, Daniel had died, too.

Her mother had tried to talk to her, explain. But by that time, it was too late. Claire had refused to listen.

The facts spoke for themselves.

She fell back on her mother's bed and lay staring up at the ceiling. The threatening tears could no longer be squeezed back and slid down her cheeks, dampening the coverlet on which she lay.

As far as she was concerned, Daniel had fallen off the face of the earth.

She'd had no idea of the degradation and humiliation he'd suffered. She wondered if those years he'd "fallen off the face of the earth" had been spent in prison, as Billy suspected.

No wonder he identified so strongly with the plight of the Japanese. Who better than he knew the sacrifices they'd made?

She'd been wrong to turn her back on him. He was an honorable man. She'd known his values and his virtues. She should have found out more.

She breathed a deep sigh and sat up.

If only he'd explained.

She still didn't know whether she agreed with his decision, but at last she understood his reasons for making it. He deserved to know that.

She gathered up the scattered letters and returned them neatly to their box. All but the last one.

It broke her heart to think how alone he must have felt, abandoned by everyone, including his own family. Yet if, as Billy had suggested, Daniel had been doing the Lord's work, he had not been alone.

In these last years, when hate and prejudice had corroded her own soul, she had forgotten that.

Billy's letter had served as a poignant reminder, forcing her to finally acknowledge the pain she had caused Daniel, to say nothing of the misery she'd created for herself.

It was a sad day, but one with a small glimmer of hope.

She would ask Daniel's forgiveness for not trusting him. He would forgive her. He was that kind of man.

But it would always be there between them. Her unwillingness to understand, the arrogance of his own expectations of her.

Her gaze fell on her mother's Bible lying on the bedside table.

The good old Bible.

She reached over and picked it up. Sitting on the edge of the bed, she let the pages fall open to the book of Psalms:

> *Let my soul live, and it shall praise thee; and let thy judgments help me. I have gone astray like a lost sheep; seek thy servant; for I do not forget thy commandments.*

Who was she to know what was in Daniel's mind? It was time she turned the matter over to God to sort through. Let the hurt go, and the blame, and the guilt.

A peace came over her and an assurance that, like Daniel, she was not alone. As she continued to read her mother's Bible, every page reflected a very human need for help and understanding for the oppressed and for sinners like her. The source of truth was timeless and as significant for her now as the day it was written.

In time, she closed the book. She had reached her decision. She knew what to do.

At that moment the telephone rang in the den.

Helen answered and a minute later stuck her head in the bedroom. "It's for you."

The rhythm of Claire's heart accelerated. Could it be Daniel? That happened sometimes when you were thinking about someone. "Who is it?"

"It's Daisy."

Her heart lagged as she moved toward the den but lifted when she heard her friend's cheerful voice.

"Helen said you're going through your mother's things. I told you I wanted to help."

"Don't worry. You'll get your chance. We're stopping for today, anyway."

"Good, then I can take you both to lunch at the club and baby shopping."

Claire covered the phone and called to Helen in the dining room. "She wants to take us to lunch and go baby shopping afterward."

"Tell her thanks, but I can't. I've got to take my mother to the doctor this afternoon."

"She can't come; her mother has a doctor's appointment."

"Alternate plan B," Daisy said. "How about I pick you up around two? We can do our shopping and meet Jack for dinner."

"Sounds fine to me," Claire said. "See you then."

Daisy's jolt of good spirits was always a welcome respite.

In the meantime, Claire posted an envelope addressed to Daniel. She enclosed Billy's letter along with a note that read, "I'm beginning to understand. Claire."

twenty-seven

Claire's friend Daisy drove as she lived, with spontaneous eccentricity and eternal trust.

Approaching a signal, she screeched to slow, then spun her yellow convertible to the right, accelerating as she rounded the corner.

Claire gripped the seat. "The Lord may be on your side, dear, but please, slow down."

"You're right. I'm sorry."

Daisy jammed her foot on the brake, throwing Claire forward, her hands braced against the dashboard.

"Oops." She gave Claire a guilty grin.

"Don't look at me. Look at the road."

"I get to talking and forget how fast I'm going," Daisy said, slowing to a more reasonable speed—which didn't affect her mouth. "As I was about to say, we've lost Vergie Parrott."

"Oh, no," Claire exclaimed. "How awful."

"She's not dead. Actually, it's very good news, if only because she's escaped from her mother's tentacles. Not that Mavis doesn't have the best of intentions—"

"Watch the road," Claire reminded her as Daisy drifted toward the right.

"Anyway," Daisy continued, "during the war, when Vergie was working at the USO, she met a nice young sailor. They've been corresponding ever since." She sped up to make it through a yellow light then resumed, for her, a more sedate pace. "Three days ago, Sam, her young man, flew into town and proposed. Vergie accepted, and last night Jack performed a sweet little ceremony for just the two of them with

154

Mrs. Beemer and me as witnesses."

"Where was her mother?"

"Refused to attend."

"How sad," Claire said, scanning the street as if she were at the wheel, her feet planted tight to the floorboard.

"Isn't it? I certainly intend to be a more sensitive, understanding, supportive mother for this little one." Daisy lowered a hand from the steering wheel and patted her very slightly bulging tummy. "Anyway, this morning I dropped the newlyweds at the airport to catch a plane for New York."

Claire smiled. "So Vergie Parrott finally flew the coop."

"I was about to say that." Daisy grinned. "But here's the clincher, Sam's an artist—"

"Hardly Mavis's occupation of choice."

"Hardly. In fact, the old gal had her eye on Jack for Vergie, before I caught him. . . . I'm not finished. Sam's last name is Bird—"

"Vergie Parrott Bird. Very good." Claire laughed.

"And they'll be living in a loft in Greenwich Village."

"Without a guest room, I'll bet."

"Anyway, as far as I can tell, he's a sweet young man, he loves Vergie, and she loves him."

"So everyone's living happily ever after except Mother Mavis."

"Who wouldn't be happy no matter what." Daisy pulled into an empty slot in the Walster's Department Store parking lot. "End of story."

"You're timing was perfect."

As she bounced out of the car, Daisy said, "Jack and I have already been looking at baby things. But you know men. He would have bought everything in fifteen minutes just to get it over with. And only what he thought was absolutely necessary." She made a face. "That's no fun."

Daisy was an heiress whose personal needs were almost as imperative and expansive as her generosity for the less fortunate—which encompassed the needs of just about the whole community.

"I like to ponder, then purchase." She turned and gave Claire a hug. "I'm so glad you came with me. It's such fun to have a girlfriend to share moments like this with."

"I'm glad, too," Claire said, hugging her back.

"I hate to think of your returning to Washington." Daisy looped her arm through Claire's.

"Don't worry. As long as you keep the sheets changed in the guest room, I'll be back for visits. I need my dose of Daisy from time to time." She patted her friend's very slightly bulging tummy. "Besides, I'm going to have to keep track of the wee one."

From the moment they pushed through the double glass doors of Walster's Department Store, the rest of the afternoon was spent focused on baby cribs and changing tables and baby carriages and diaper hampers. . . .

Claire wondered if she'd ever have any better use for diapers than as dusting cloths.

Oh, how she hoped so.

"Naturally I'll have a diaper service," Daisy said.

And delivery blankets and booties and. . .

"My color of choice is pink, of course," Daisy said, lifting a tiny blue shirt. "But what if she's a boy?"

"There are always stripes." Claire pointed out a pink-and-blue-striped crib fender with matching coverlet and pillows.

And bassinets and sweet little baby sheets with flower faces on them. . .

"Don't get everything now," Claire said. "Before I go back to Washington, I intend to give you a baby shower."

"Oh, that's so sweet." Daisy squeezed her hand.

But by the time the store closed, which was upon their exit, it looked like Daisy had ordered or purchased everything the baby would need until the age of six.

"You forgot its school lunch pail," Claire quipped as she got into the seat on the passenger side and slammed the door.

Daisy looked stricken. "I did?"

"I was just kidding."

"So was I."

"Uh-huh."

"Jack's really going to get a shock when it's all delivered," Daisy said. "That'll make him sit up and take notice. He still can't believe we're expecting."

"We?"

"You know what I mean."

Indeed Claire did. Daisy and Jack were in this together and would share all the joy and even some of the pain— Claire was sure Daisy would provide Jack with a play by play of that, too.

Daisy glanced at the clock on the dashboard. "Oh, dear. We're going to be late." She turned the key in the ignition. "Oh well, it won't hurt the boys to entertain each other for a few minutes."

"The boys?" Claire felt a rush of apprehension.

Daisy glanced over at her. "Daniel will be joining us."

"I wish you'd told me."

"Would it have made a difference?"

"It might have."

"Daniel seemed pleased when he knew you'd be coming."

"He did? That's good."

"Okay?"

Claire gave her a sheepish smile. "Sure."

Daisy backed out of the parking spot and spun toward the exit, then out into the street.

Would it have made a difference? Indeed it would. Claire would have tried to put the dinner part of this little jaunt off—at least until she knew Daniel had received Billy's letter.

Now how was she supposed to behave?

It would be hard to act natural. After finding the letter, all she wanted to do was apologize and get it over with before she went back to Washington.

"You look fabulous in that plum dress, Claire. And the avocado trim on the jacket matches your hat perfectly. I love it."

Subtle, Daisy was not.

"You don't need to placate me, Daisy." Claire crossed her arms. "I'm not upset. At least not about this evening. Your driving, maybe. Anyway, I anticipate a very pleasant time." She glanced at her friend. "Although don't think I'm so naive as not to know what you're up to."

"What do you mean?" Daisy assumed a look of innocence.

"Setting up Daniel and me, as if you didn't know." Claire smoothed her white suede glove. "Where are we going for dinner?"

"The Gold Room. Jack made the reservation."

"That's spiffy."

"The best for the best," Daisy said, driving beneath the front awning of the hotel and pulling to a stop. "The boys will be meeting us in the lobby."

Two attendants in white uniforms helped Daisy and Claire from the car, and two liveried doormen held open the imposing carved teak doors as they strode into the elegantly appointed lobby. The cavernous room teamed with weary travelers in wrinkled jackets, regular folks like themselves out for an evening on the town, and socialites in sequined gowns escorted by tuxedoed gentlemen heading for a special event in the ballroom.

Their voices and laughter melded with the sharp clang of a bell on the check-in desk and the beat of a jazz pianist in the corner surrounded by potted palms and round tables for two.

"There they are," Daisy cried, spotting Jack and Daniel not far from the entrance.

The two men stood up as Claire and Daisy approached.

Meeting Daniel's gaze, Claire's heart throbbed, remembering the whispering caress of his lips and how she'd ached to have his arms around her.

She lowered her eyes, struggling to mask the longing she feared she would reveal.

Daisy ran ahead. She threw her arms around Jack and on tiptoe, planted a swift, resounding kiss on his lips. She pulled back and laughed up into his eyes, then turning, gave Daniel's cheek an affectionate pat.

Oh, how Claire envied Daisy her unself-conscious ardor, her spontaneous abandon.

"Have you boys been waiting long?" Daisy asked, linking her arm through Jack's. "When is the reservation? I hope they don't put us near the kitchen."

"Don't worry, they won't." He grinned at her. "I took care of it like you taught me."

Claire looked over and found herself meeting Daniel's disconcerting gaze again. He studied her with intent interest, yet there was a reticence in his eyes.

What did he see in hers?

He stepped forward. "Claire." He spoke her name almost as a question, as if he were not quite sure how she would respond.

Around her, the noise of the crowd, the voices faded. Even Daisy's lilting tones were muted as he drew closer. He took her hand, and she saw her own longing reflected in his gaze.

❧

The elegant ambience of the Gold Room was wasted on Claire. The two tiers of banquettes, the flickering candles and fresh flowers, the crystal chandeliers, even the music from the wandering musicians were consigned to the farthest corner of her brain, she was so achingly aware of Daniel's hand at her elbow.

A small gesture that sent shivers up her spine.

As she climbed the steps to the second tier, her feet hardly touched the floor; she felt fresh as a starry-eyed debutante with her first love, all tingly and anxious.

This was ridiculous. *Grow up!*

She was a thirty-one-year-old woman with a disrupted past and an uncertain future.

More than likely she had seen in Daniel's eyes only what she'd wanted to see, a reflection of her own feelings, not his.

Oh, how she wished he'd already received Billy's letter and her note, then she wouldn't have to speculate or surmise or fantasize. His eyes, his words would tell her.

The men were seated on either end of the banquette, Daisy and Claire between them.

"Once the baby's here, we won't be having evenings like this very often," Daisy said.

Jack picked up his menu. "We have nearly six months to go, Daisy. There's still time."

Daisy gave Claire a smug smile. "See, I told you it was 'we.'" She leaned close to Jack and squeezed his arm. "Isn't this fun, our all being together like this?" Without looking at Claire, she said, "I'm trying to convince my friend not to go back to Washington. This is where she belongs. All in favor say aye."

"Please, no," Claire burst out before they could respond. "Daisy, please."

"I'm sorry, Claire." Daisy looked almost chastened as she pulled her napkin into her lap. "But there's nothing for you in Washington that you can't accomplish here, and you're one of our best friends, and we don't want to live without you. Do we?" She glanced at Daniel.

Jack frowned. "Daisy."

Even he could see how embarrassingly blatant she was being.

But she would not be deterred. "Well? Am I right?" she asked Daniel, waiting for his response.

"Claire will do what she needs to do," Daniel said.

That was fast.

Well, there was her answer. There was reality. Daniel obviously was not set on her staying.

"But we'll miss her if she chooses to go," he added quietly.

Were her ears deceiving her, or was she once again hearing what she chose to hear?

"You're absolutely right," Daisy exclaimed. "See Claire?"

Claire glanced at Daniel, who returned a helpless shrug and a benign smile.

Hard to be more noncommittal than that.

No promises there.

Friends. That was the best it would be. Probably the best it should be.

The waiter came to take their order, blessedly diverting their attention.

"You must have the *Coquilles St. Jacques à la Provençale*, Claire. It's superb here," Daisy said.

"That sounds lovely." And it saved Claire from having to make a decision.

Even though scallops sautéed the French way were one of Claire's favorite dishes, she hardly tasted them as she went through the motions of eating and making conversation.

Of course, Daisy had to notice.

"You're hardly touching your dinner, dear. Aren't you feeling well?"

Claire was saved from having to respond by a young couple who had suddenly approached their table.

The man was of medium height and broad build with red hair and wearing a dark suit. He looked about ten years younger than Jack and Daniel. The young woman beside him was in Daisy's favorite pink from head to toe. An outfit that looked decidedly new. She stood close enough to the young man for no light to show between them, and her pink-gloved hand clung to his as if they had been glued.

"Newlyweds," Daisy whispered under her breath.

"Excuse me," the young man said, looking straight at Daniel. "Aren't you Sergeant Essex?"

twenty-eight

Sergeant?

Claire glanced at Daniel, who suddenly looked very tense.

"If you aren't Sergeant Essex, you're a dead ringer," the young man said.

"I think you've made a mistake," Daisy said.

Daniel slowly stood up. "I'm Sergeant Essex."

Daisy let out a protracted sigh, as if all the air was being squeezed from her lungs.

What was going on here?

"I'm Eddy Freeman, Sergeant. Corporal Eddy Freeman." The young man grabbed Daniel's hand and shook it fiercely. "We were in the same battalion, remember?"

"What's this all about?" Daisy whispered.

"You tell me." Claire glanced over at Jack, who looked just as confused.

Daniel's face lit with recognition. "Of course I remember you, Eddy. How are you? You look well." He smiled at the young woman beside him. "I can see why."

"My wife, Ragene," the corporal said proudly. "Got hitched last week. We're on our honeymoon."

"I can always spot them," Daisy murmured.

"Well, congratulations."

"I wouldn't be here if it wasn't for you, Sergeant."

"Come on, Eddy." Daniel looked embarrassed. "Let me introduce my friends, Miss Middlebrook and the Reverend and Mrs. McCutcheon."

Claire struggled for a gracious smile. After all, it wasn't

the young man's fault he'd just opened a can of worms.

Jack began to rise.

"Please, don't get up," the corporal said. "I just wanted my wife to meet the man who saved my life." He turned back to Daniel. "I can't believe it. What a wedding present, seeing you." He dropped his wife's hand and threw his arms around Daniel, slapping his back in a manly embrace.

Suddenly he pulled away and drew a handkerchief from his back pocket. He wiped his eyes and blew his nose. "Sorry, seeing you. . ."

You needn't have bothered bringing your own, Claire thought. *Daniel carries a spare.*

He shoved the handkerchief back into his pocket and grabbed his wife's hand again. "This is the man, honey."

Ragene gave Daniel a shy smile. "Eddy's told me a lot about you."

"I can't believe meeting up with you like this." His glance skirted the booth. "This man is the bravest of the brave."

Claire glanced at Daniel. He hadn't looked in her direction since the couple had appeared.

Even though the corporal claimed they were not staying, it was obvious that before they moved on, he was determined to share his story. All of it.

"In the beginning, the guys who were COs, conscientious objectors, really got it. I mean bad. 'Cause they refused to carry a weapon." Eddy shook his head. "But all it took was one battle, and everybody was calling 'em doc. Always at the front, in the thick of things. Men dropping like flies around 'em, but if a guy had breath, the medic never left him."

Daniel was a medic?

Eddy paused, his voice quiet. "I got mine at Anzio. The

Jerries wouldn't let up. They were all over us. I got hit right off. Would have died right there on that beach, a million miles from home, but for Sergeant Essex. He wouldn't leave me. Stayed right there 'til he could get me back to the aid station. Carried me on his back a hundred yards at least. Bullets flying. I don't know how he made it. God must have been on his side. And soon as he got me on the litter, he turned right around and went back. No gun, no nothin'. Nothin' but his medic bag."

The others at the table may have been dumbstruck, but the more Claire heard, the angrier she got.

"Sorry I interrupted your party, folks." Eddie smiled, slightly embarrassed. "But I couldn't let this pass. I had to say thank you one more time."

Daniel put his hand on the younger man's shoulder. "Don't thank me. We all had our jobs to do."

Right.

Claire knew she should be admiring Daniel's bravery, his modesty, but all she could think was, *Why didn't you tell me?*

"I'll never forget you, Sergeant Essex."

"Nor I, you, Eddy."

Nor this remarkably enlightening evening, Claire thought.

The two men shook hands.

Eddy said, "Nice meeting you, folks. And don't you forget: You're sittin' with a hero."

Maybe on the battlefront but not in his own backyard. Claire moved as far from Daniel as possible as he slid into the seat next to her. She was too angry to look at him or speak.

As soon as the newlyweds had left, Daisy leaned across the table. "Why didn't you tell us, Daniel?"

"I guess because I was so angry." Daniel crossed his

arms. "I was still the same person even if I had decided to be a conscientious objector. I didn't condemn others for their choices, but I was condemned for mine. It seemed as if everyone I knew had passed judgment."

Did he say that for her benefit? Judgment about what? If she'd judged, she'd judged on what she knew, which, as it turned out, was next to nothing.

If they hadn't been in a public place, if they hadn't been with Daisy and Jack, Claire would have let him have it.

"Even my family considered me a disgrace. Everybody's mind was already made up. So what was the point?"

Claire could tell him. How about trust? How about sharing?

"Most people still don't know what we did," Daniel said.

"Well, at least now we know what *you* did." Claire spoke for the first time, her voice taut with anger.

Daisy caught it. "I'm surprised you haven't had more to say," she whispered.

"I'm saving it."

"Hush, Daisy," Jack said gently. "Daniel's talking."

Now that the war was over and it didn't matter, he was willing to explain it all.

High time.

"We were medics, like I was, or ambulance drivers with the American Field Service. Some of us worked in medical clinics and mental hospitals or served as human guinea pigs in medical experiments."

It seemed that Corporal Eddy Freeman's appearance had suddenly broken the dam of Daniel's restraint and an emotional deluge rushed forth. "We built roads and dams. One of the most dangerous jobs was as smoke jumpers. Those were the men who parachuted into the hotspots during forest fires." Daniel frowned. "They faced two foes: the flames and the character assassins waiting back at camp. And most of them worked for nothing. No money. No benefits for the men or their families. They put their lives on the line, too, but without guns."

He took a deep breath. "Yes, I was angry."

"It sounds as if you still are," Daisy said. "Not that I blame you."

It had been awful what they had gone through. What Daniel had gone through. There was no denying that. But one thing had nothing to do with the other. He had not leveled with her. Not from the very beginning.

Claire wanted to feel sorry for him. And she did. She knew he had suffered. But more than ever, she was realizing his part of the responsibility for destroying their relationship. It was he who had not been forthright and honest.

The blame was not all with her. There was plenty to go around.

And it was time he knew it.

Needless to say, Claire didn't intend to linger over coffee.

twenty-nine

Since Daniel had driven Jack to the hotel and Daisy had driven Claire, they switched for the ride home.

Daniel's car barely made it out of the parking lot before Claire lit into him.

"How could you? How could you not tell me that you were a medic? You may see yourself as brave, long-suffering, noble, pure, a knight in shining armor who nobody understands or appreciates"—she paused for a gulp of air—"but I don't."

"I never said—"

"*You never said* is right. You never said anything. I was supposedly the woman you loved, that you wanted to spend the rest of your life with, and you didn't trust me enough to share the most obvious facts of your life."

"Claire—"

"Don't *Claire* me. You had your chance; now it's mine. What did you think, that I was some fatuous lightweight who didn't have the brains to reason it out? That I should just blindly go along with anything you wanted to do without knowing what or why? Well, that's not the woman I was, and that's not the woman I am now."

"Simmer down, Claire."

"Simmer down! Your arrogance has no limits. For five long years I've been living with regrets and bitterness. You destroyed our love. You destroyed our future. And I'm supposed to simmer down?"

"Look, Claire, you knew the kind of man I was—"

"Oh, I did? Oh really? Hardly. If tonight was any indication. Why. . .why, you confided more in my brother than you did in me, your fiancée. But you even left him hanging."

She let out a sigh of frustration. She wasn't through. She was just catching her breath.

"I found a letter from Billy in my mother's things. He explained what you and he went through. You were the brave one, he said. You were the hero." She took a deep, shuddering breath and let it out slowly. "I sent it to you. I also enclosed a note saying I was beginning to understand." She balled her hand into a fist. "Well, scratch that. After tonight, I've changed my mind. I don't understand you at all."

"What would you have said if I had confided in you?" Daniel asked.

Claire was quiet for a moment. "I don't know. That was before Billy died. I hope. . .I think I would have understood, honored your decision." She looked over at him. "Stuck by you. I loved you that much." She shrugged and looked out the window. "But we'll never know, will we?"

By now they had reached her home. Daniel pulled into the driveway.

"Don't bother to see me in." She opened the car door and stepped out, slamming it behind her.

The car stayed in the driveway, the headlights beaming on her as she extracted her key from her purse and unlocked the front door, entered and closed it behind her.

She leaned back against it, waiting until she heard the shift of gears and the crunch of tires rolling over the dried sycamore leaves.

The house was still. By now, Helen had gone to bed.

Claire was alone.

She might as well get used to it.

She wondered if she'd ever love another man the way she had loved Daniel.

She'd said what she had to say.

Did she feel better for it?

Tomorrow she'd know. Tonight she was numb.

Numb and bone-weary.

Suddenly so weary that she could hardly draw one foot after the other.

She didn't turn on the light in her room but dropped onto the bed. She kicked off her shoes and laid her hat and gloves on the quilt next to her, then lay back and closed her eyes, struggling to sort it all out and finally too tired to try.

The shrill, insistent ring of the alarm clock woke her.

Her eyes flew open.

It was still dark.

She squinted at the lighted face of the clock.

The hands were at two thirty.

It rang again.

It wasn't the alarm. It was the doorbell.

She turned on the light next to her bed.

A thief wouldn't ring the doorbell.

Still bleary from sleep, she stumbled from her bedroom into the hall.

Who else would it be but. . .

"Who is it?"

"It's me."

She hesitated. "Me?" As if she didn't know.

"Me, Daniel. I need to talk to you."

She didn't answer.

"Claire, please."

Let him stand out there and freeze.

"I'm not leaving until you talk to me."

She imagined him on the other side of the double oak door, determined, shaking in the chill air.

Her resolve began to thaw. "Do you know what time it is?"

"Two thirty. It's freezing out here. Open the door, Claire. You know you're going to eventually."

"What makes you so sure?" The cad always could read her mind.

She leaned against the doorjamb.

"You're a journalist. Curious. It's in your blood. You always go for the big story."

She lifted her hand but didn't turn the knob. "You call this the big story?"

"It is to me." His voice was quiet.

She had to press her ear against the crack between the double doors to make out what he said. With each soft-spoken word, her heart picked up pace.

She at least owed him a listen.

But she wasn't going to make it easy.

She turned on the porch light and twisted the deadbolt.

Finally, she opened the door.

Daniel stood in the glow, as tall and handsomely appealing as he'd ever looked, his expressive face filled with emotion, his dark eyes burning.

She didn't say anything, just stepped aside and let him enter, then closed the door behind him and turned on the hall light. This was as far into the house as he was going to get.

At least for now.

He stood before her in the brightened entry, twisting his fedora between his fingers.

She crossed her arms. "Well?"

"You were right, Claire." He swallowed. "I should have

trusted the woman I loved instead of indulging my typical male ego and pride." He shifted his weight and lowered his eyes. "But. . .here I am, my hat in my hand"—his gaze lifted—"and my heart on my sleeve."

She remembered the first time he'd proposed, in the fresh, scented air beside the stream: *"I'll be a good husband, Claire. I'll take care of you, and always be faithful. . . ."*

Her heart pounded. A lump rose in her throat.

His voice was husky and uncertain. "Oh, Claire, if you'll have me, I'll spend the rest of my life making it up to you."

"Only a lifetime?" she murmured.

Her man of few words had finally found the right ones.

"Well," she sighed, "that should be good for a start," and smiled as she allowed him to draw her into his arms.

epilogue

There didn't seem a point to a big wedding. Claire had no family left, and Daniel's parents had chosen not to cancel their scheduled cruise.

"Their loss," Claire said and kissed him. "We're our own family now."

They were married in a quiet ceremony in the sanctuary of the Good Shepherd Community Church with Jack officiating, Daisy and Helen as witnesses, and Mrs. Beemer at the organ.

Claire wore traditional white and a locket that had belonged to her mother. She carried flowers Daisy had picked from the Fielding estate.

The honeymoon came after Claire had sent her piece on the Japanese to Larry, her editor at *Life*. She and Daniel picked up a copy of the magazine in the airport on their way home from Hawaii. A picture of Helen and her adopted daughter, Sara, was on the cover of that week's issue.

As Daniel engulfed Claire in a proud hug, she offered a silent prayer of thanks for God's grace and manifold blessings.

historical notes

A few people living in the internment camps were not Japanese: husbands who accompanied wives and wives who accompanied husbands. Ralph Lazo, an American of Mexican-Irish descent, chose to go with his Japanese American friends to Manzanar. Subsequently, he was drafted and later awarded a Bronze Star for heroism in combat.

Some Japanese felt that, despite the injustices of internment, the camps saved lives that might have been taken as a result of the extreme prejudice of the times. Among those was S. I. Hawakawa (1906–92), American educator and U.S. senator from California (1977–82). Hawakawa served as a president of San Francisco State University and founded a lobbying organization dedicated to making English the official language of the United States.

On February 8, 2000, fifty-five years late, President Bill Clinton presented the Medal of Honor to twenty-two brave Japanese American soldiers who had fought in World War II. Of the twenty-two given, fifteen of the medals were presented posthumously.

In 2003, the Torrance National Guard Armory was named after the wartime hero, Ted Tanouye. The following year, a memorial in his honor was unveiled across the street from his alma mater, Torrance High School, from which he graduated in 1938.

A Letter To Our Readers

Dear Readers:

   In order that we might better contribute to your reading enjoyment, we would appreciate your taking a few minutes to respond to the following questions. We welcome your comments and read each form and letter we receive. When completed, please return to the following:

Fiction Editor
Heartsong Presents
PO Box 719
Uhrichsville, Ohio 44683

1. Did you enjoy reading *Against the Tide* by Rachel Druten?
   ❑ Very much! I would like to see more books by this author!
   ❑ Moderately. I would have enjoyed it more if

   _____

   _____

   _____

2. Are you a member of **Heartsong Presents?** ❑ Yes ❑ No
   If no, where did you purchase this book? _____

   _____

3. How would you rate, on a scale from 1 (poor) to 5 (superior), the cover design? _____

4. On a scale from 1 (poor) to 10 (superior), please rate the following elements.
   _____ Heroine   _____ Plot
   _____ Hero   _____ Inspirational theme
   _____ Setting   _____ Secondary characters

5. These characters were special because? _____

_____

_____

6. How has this book inspired your life? _____

_____

_____

7. What settings would you like to see covered in future
   Heartson Presents books? _____

_____

_____

8. What are some inspirational themes you would like to see
   treated in future books? _____

_____

_____

9. Would you be interested in reading other **Heartsong
   Presents** titles? ❑ Yes   ❑ No

10.   Please check your age range:

   ❑ Under 18   ❑ 18–24
   ❑ 25–34   ❑ 35–45
   ❑ 46–55   ❑ Over 55

Name _____
Occupation _____
Address _____